Kate watched him as she took a large mouthful of wine, her eyes filled with a longing he dared not put a name to.

He took a sip of his drink and placed the glass on the table beside him, not looking away from Kate's gaze for a second.

Kate leaned sideways and put her glass down, too, still watching him.

Simultaneously they reached for each other, their mouths meeting, touching, tasting, feeding that longing he'd seen in her eyes and known inside his heart. This was Kate, the woman who'd played with his mind for months, the woman he'd kissed once before and never forgotten what it had felt like. *Kate*. He tightened his hold around her, drew her even closer so her breasts were pressed against his chest, her stomach pushing into him. She was wonderful.

Dear Reader,

Having a young springer spaniel who manages to get into all sorts of trouble, I've spent a bit of time with vets lately. They and their nurses are so wonderful with the animals that come under their care, and hence I decided to write a story involving vets.

Kate has huge issues with scarring on her body that has caused the few men she's let close to walk away, leaving her sad and unable to trust. When she meets Finn, he sets her alight on the inside—until he, too, walks away.

Months later, they find themselves working together and the sparks are flying again. Kate has to work hard to keep control over her emotions. So does Finn. But sometimes hearts have a mind of their own, and these two have more to work through than just being vets in the same clinic.

I hope you enjoy reading how they resolve their issues on the way to love.

Sue MacKay

BROODING VET FOR THE WALLFLOWER

SUE MACKAY

MEDICAL ROMANCE

Harlequin®
MEDICAL ROMANCE

ISBN-13: 978-1-335-94273-9

Brooding Vet for the Wallflower

Harlequin Enterprises ULC
22 Adelaide St. West, 41st Floor
Toronto, Ontario M5H 4E3, Canada
www.Harlequin.com

Printed in U.S.A.

Sue MacKay lives with her husband in New Zealand's beautiful Marlborough Sounds, with the water on her doorstep and the birds and the trees at her back door. It is the perfect setting to indulge her passions of entertaining friends by cooking them sumptuous meals, drinking fabulous wine, going for hill walks or kayaking around the bay—and, of course, writing stories.

Books by Sue MacKay

Harlequin Medical Romance

Queenstown Search & Rescue

Captivated by Her Runaway Doc
A Single Dad to Rescue Her
From Best Friends to I Do?

Fling with Her Long-Lost Surgeon
Stranded with the Paramedic
Single Mom's New Year Wish
Brought Together by a Pup
Fake Fiancée to Forever?
Resisting the Pregnant Pediatrician
Marriage Reunion with the Island Doc
Paramedic's Fling to Forever
Healing the Single Dad Surgeon

Visit the Author Profile page
at Harlequin.com for more titles.

This story is dedicated to those who
care for sick animals. You people rock.

CHAPTER ONE

'KATE, YOU HAVEN'T had the privilege of meeting one of our past colleagues, Finn Anderson.' Jackson gave him a cheeky grin. 'Finn, this is one of our vets, Kate Phillips.'

Finn knew his friend well enough to know from the look in his eyes that he had ideas about how well he and Kate might get along. As far as he was concerned, Jackson could think again. It wasn't happening. He was only back home for his brother's wedding before returning to Scotland and his fantastic job there in a fortnight's time. He was not looking for a new relationship. The last one hadn't gone cold yet, and the lessons learned would probably prevent that from ever happening. He was not open to sharing his life and all he'd worked for ever again. As for his heart—that was locked down as tight as possible.

As he turned to meet the woman standing beside Jackson, his stomach dropped. Never had he seen such a beautiful woman. Classic features enhanced by long, straight, strawberry-blonde hair and drag-him-under fudge-brown eyes. Then there was the figure to die for. Surely she came with a warning tag? Like a serious warning about how he would combust if he touched her, or even stood too close to her.

Kate looked at him and said, 'Hello, Finn. I mightn't have met you but I've heard a bit about you.'

'Hello, Kate. Yes, I seem to remember there're times when Jackson does exceed the sensible levels of idle chatter.' Especially when he was on a mission to interfere in his friend's life, as he had been ever since it had gone down the gutter more than three years ago. All Finn could hope for was that Jackson would continue to keep his trap shut about his past. His pal might be a pain about some things, but he felt certain he could trust him on that one. It was his story to share, no one else's, and he had no intentions of doing that with anybody. Not even a stunning woman who had him looking twice to see if she was for real. Which she most certainly was.

'Yeah, right.' Jackson grinned.

Finn stepped closer and said quietly, 'Knock it off, pal.' This was his first time home to New Zealand in nearly two years and next time he took a break from work he intended exploring parts of France. Yet he had to admit it felt surprisingly good to be here. He couldn't be ready to return home, surely? It was good to catch up with friends but returning permanently wasn't yet an option.

He was still getting over how his fiancée, an accountant to boot, had bankrupted them. Not them so much as him, because she hadn't had any finances to begin with. It had been a terrible time facing up to what she'd done and dealing with the resulting consequences. The money she'd told him she'd spent on wedding plans had instead been sucked up at the casino, along with lots more that she'd shrugged off as their living expenses. There'd even been a loan he'd known nothing about until the bank had foreclosed on it and started the whole process that had seen him left with little more than the clothes he'd stood up in. He'd lost his veterinary business, wasn't allowed a loan of any kind for four years, and all the money he'd earned since had gone to paying back debtors even though he wasn't obligated to do so.

Living on the other side of the world was helping to put it all behind him, but not the fact he'd struggle to ever again trust someone with the things that mattered most to him. Love, family, and working for his own pleasure and gain. Not only had Amelia financially ruined him, she'd broken his heart. She'd been the love of his life. He might've forgiven her if she'd been willing to do something about her gambling problem, but she'd laughed at that idea, saying it wasn't a problem and she could stop any time she chose. Nor had she once apologised for ruining everything for him.

She'd also stolen from clients of the accounting firm she'd worked for and consequently had her accreditation taken away. Harder to swallow was that a year ago she'd married a wealthy man and had recently had a baby. That news had torn him further apart because it had shown how far she'd go to set herself up for life. Telling him she was pregnant when it had been an out and out lie had been the final kick in the guts for him because she'd actually shown him a positive test strip she'd got from a pregnant friend. All to keep him at her side until she'd found someone else to give her the lifestyle she craved, and that the casino hadn't provided. To think he'd fallen hard and fast for her, and had no idea who she really was. Once bitten, so the saying went, the rest of which was now his motto.

'Relax, Finn.' Jackson brought him back to the here and now, probably well aware of where he'd gone. 'This is a party. You're meant to be enjoying yourself catching up with old friends.'

He couldn't argue with that. The Lincoln Vet Clinic staff were in a room at the pub to celebrate winning clinic of the year for their work with the racehorses bred and trained around Lincoln and when they'd heard he was in town they'd made sure he came along. 'It's great seeing everyone.' He glanced at Kate.

And meeting new people.

Down, man. He wasn't staying around after the wedding.

'You're a local?'

She smiled. 'Cantabrian through and through.'

That smile could wreck any intentions to remain aloof. He took a step back. 'It's not a bad place to live. I do miss certain aspects.' On the days when he forgot why he'd left in the first place, and, face it, those days were rare. The humiliation over what Amelia had done was never far from the surface, along with the pain in his heart. Throw in his complete lack of trust and he was a screw-up.

'You don't intend returning home?' Kate asked.

'Not in the foreseeable future. The job I'm doing is too good an opportunity to toss it aside.' More importantly, he needed to stay away until he'd totally sorted his head out and knew how he was going to move on from the past. Might be years before that happened.

When he and Amelia had first got together, it had been wonderful. It hadn't bothered him that she'd wanted to live in Wellington where she'd grown up. It was natural to support his partner, right? She'd had a good job with a top company in the CBD and he had been happy to set up a veterinary practice on the edge of the city. Little had he known what he was letting himself in for when she'd suggested she look after the financial side of his business He hadn't had a clue that she knew what she was doing in more ways than legal when it came to rigging the books. Nor had he known about her gambling habit until it was too late. Her greed had got in the way of honesty. It wasn't as though she'd been raised in poverty. Her parents were hard-working and did well with their grocery business.

'What field are you working in?' Kate asked.

'I'm working for a rural practice that deals big time with Aberdeen cattle breeders.'

'Bet that's interesting.'

'It is.' Those eyes were sucking him in too easily. He took another step back.

Jackson nudged him. 'Let's join everyone else and get closer to the fire.'

'Good idea.' Winter was making itself felt today, though not a patch on the winters he'd experienced in Scotland. They were something else. Just thinking about them made him shiver.

He shook himself mentally and glanced at the beautiful woman before him. His skin tingled, making him all hot and bothered. How was he going to get through the evening and come out sane? Because he wasn't coming out any other way. Until now he'd believed it was a given that he stayed clear of temptation as the consequences could be destructive and he wasn't prepared to take that risk again.

'I'll get a drink first. Would you like one, Kate?' Hopefully the barman would take an hour to pour the drinks, giving him time to settle back to normal. Looking at Kate as he waited for her answer, he felt a surge of pure lust strike. She really should be on the cover of a fashion magazine. But then, for all he knew, she might already be.

'G and T, thanks.'

'Me, too,' Jackson called over his shoulder.

Finn headed to the bar, unable to shake Kate from his mind. She was something else. Beautiful beyond words, yet she didn't come across as overly confident. Or was it that she wasn't cocky? There was a stillness about her that suggested she took no crap from anyone, and thought things through before opening her mouth. Again, he was probably wrong, because what would he know when it came to reading women? But no denying she didn't appear to be aware of her beauty in a full-on kind of way.

He was surprised at how easily she intrigued him. No woman had done that since Amelia, who he'd got involved with quickly, believing he'd found the love of his life. She'd reciprocated just as strongly. Showed how wrong he could be. Something to remember when he was sitting up and taking notice of Kate after he'd sworn off involvement of any kind other than the occasional brief fling. And that was not happening with this woman stirring his blood. He sensed she could get too close too fast and thereby hurt him. He had no idea where that came from, but he'd trust his instincts even though they'd failed him in the past with Amelia. He was clear he wasn't setting himself up for a fall.

Just as well he was home for only a short period. That'd save him making an idiot of himself, along with getting Jackson off his back. Jackson had never liked Amelia and seemed determined to interfere in getting Finn back on his feet. Bring on the return flight to Britain. He needed his own space and that was impossible here in Canterbury with everyone determined to get him out amongst it and shove his ex-fiancée completely into the past. Amelia *was* his past, but the ramifications of what she'd done weren't and were unlikely to ever totally go away. There was a huge warning hanging over his head.

Remain wary.

Not hard to do. Until tonight, it seemed. That'd come right once he sorted his mind.

'I'll take those drinks to the table.' A soft feminine voice slipped through his thoughts, tightening his fingers into his palm.

There were only three glasses. 'I could've managed,' he said abruptly, then felt bad. Protecting himself came with problems. 'But thanks. Here's yours.'

Why had Kate come across to join him? Was she the kind of woman who always offered to help out? Or had he inadvertently stirred her blood too?

'Thanks.' Her smile went straight to his head. And his groin.

Too many of those and he wouldn't be able to account for anything he said or did, despite his best intentions. 'Any time.' He winced. Not any time. He wouldn't be seeing Kate after tonight, no matter what.

'Is your job permanent, or are you restricted by immigration laws?' Kate asked as they crossed to the table where Jackson was.

'Permanent. My mum's British so there was no issue when it came to applying for work over there.'

'That's handy.'

'Saves a lot of hassles, which is good. I'm not into hassles,' he added lightly, because he didn't know what else to say without getting too intense. For some reason she did that to him even

though he'd only just met her. Not a good look
if he intended remaining remote, which he had
to do for his own sake.

'Something I understand,' Kate replied. Strange
how her beauty was so out there and yet her voice
was quiet and calm, not saying look at him in any
way, unlike other women he'd met who weren't
half as beautiful. 'You like living on the other
side of the world?' she asked.

'Yes.' It put distance between him and the
past. And unfortunately his family and friends,
whom he missed a lot.

'So you don't intend returning to New Zealand any time soon?'

It was as though she was sussing him out, but
that couldn't be, surely? Or had he tweaked her
interest in the same way she'd done to him? 'No.
At the moment I'm enjoying the work, along
with the knowledge I'm acquiring, so I won't be
quitting my position in the foreseeable future.'
Time to turn the conversation off him and onto
Kate. 'What about you? Travelled a lot?'

Thought you weren't going down this track.

If he hadn't been watching her he wouldn't
have seen the shadow that crossed her face or
the sharp touch she made to her upper abdomen.
What was that about?

'Twice to Oz is my lot. I keep thinking I'll
head away on my OE one day but it never hap-

pens. Guess having a long overseas experience isn't at the top of my bucket list.'

It was something a lot of Kiwis did before settling into their careers. 'What is, then?' Why the heck did he keep asking questions when all he wanted was to put space between them?

'Making the most of my career. I love being a vet. It makes the thought of travelling seem a little redundant.'

'Are you more into domestic animal health? Or do you work rurally?' He did need to shut up or she'd be getting the wrong idea.

'I far prefer looking out for dogs and cats. Though tonight's all about horses.' She looked around the crowded room, a soft smile lighting up her beautiful face. 'I'd better mix and mingle a bit. We're meant to chat to the horse breeders as they were a big part of us winning the award.'

'No problem. I'll catch up with the guys I used to work with.'

And take a breather from wondering what it would be like to hold you in my arms.

But he was unable to take his eyes off that sensational backside covered in tight black jeans as Kate strolled away. What if he let go his restraints and had some fun for one night? It wasn't as though that'd be setting him up for a fall. He'd be back on the other side of the world in fourteen days.

But while Kate had been quick to ask him about his career, he had no idea what she might be thinking about anything else. She seemed able to keep her thoughts to herself far better than he managed. She hadn't come on to him, nor had she pushed her own veterinary knowledge to prove she was his equal, as a couple of vets he'd recently met in Scotland had done. Kate was almost too good to be true. *Almost.* No woman was that good. And if he wasn't bitter, then what was he?

Kate put her cocktail glass aside and leaned one elbow on the bar while she watched people letting loose on the dance floor. The pub had provided music for the evening and just about everyone was getting into the mood and letting their hair down. Or swinging their bodies all over the place.

If only I had the same confidence.

Unfortunately, after the put-downs she'd had about the state of her body from the few men she'd been intimate with since her marriage collapsed, she'd become ultra-cautious about showing too much of herself to anyone. Especially her horrific scars. Throw in how Hamish had gone off her and walked away as though their marriage meant nothing, and her self-confidence was rocky at the best of times. Not that she'd be exposing any part of her body while dancing, but she didn't want to attract attention. Focusing on the crowd, she admitted she'd like to have some fun without thinking about everything that had gone wrong for her. 'Everyone's gone crazy.'

Beside her, Finn laughed. 'It says a lot about the evening.'

Thoughtlessly she said, 'Think I'll try a bit of dancing,' surprising herself. Was it her way of asking him to join her? Could be, she admitted. He was quite something to look at.

He obliged. 'Want a partner for that?' Finn asked, then looked as surprised as she felt. Hadn't he meant to ask her?

Tough. At worst, they'd dance and go their separate ways. At best? She had no idea other than her fingers itched to touch him. He was so gorgeous her breathing was off beat, and she couldn't ignore him for long.

'Sure, why not?' Might as well have some fun, and forget everything else for once. Watching closely, she saw heat creep into his cheeks. What was going on? Was he as insecure as her? Had someone done the dirty on him too?

Well, buster, the night is nowhere near over and you are something else.

The usual tightness around her need to let go and relax was loosening unexpectedly. Getting up close to that muscular body would be a treat.

A few dance moves could only be good, and as he had made it clear by talking only about work that he wasn't into her, she wasn't setting herself up to be hurt further along the way.

Don't forget he'll soon be heading away again.

How could she forget when he'd talked about how much he enjoyed his life in Britain? There was nothing to fear about getting too interested in him. There wasn't enough time. A one-nighter would be the best thing for her if she followed through on the heated sensations filling her. What was wrong with having some fun and not waiting for the put-down that always came these days? What was wrong was that she didn't do it any more.

But for some inexplicable reason, Finn was getting to her in ways she didn't believe possible. Finn might even enjoy spending time up close with her. If he did notice her scars, which she'd do her utmost to prevent, he might be the first man in a long time not to reject her, though she knew she was dreaming there. After the last failed attempt at a relationship because the guy couldn't handle the mess her body was, she'd come to the conclusion it would be wise to run solo and forget trying to find that special someone to trust with her love, so her heart would remain intact.

Yet here she was, considering a short fling—

a one-off and not a relationship—which said a lot about how much Finn was getting to her. He was the sexiest man she'd met in ages. What was there to lose other than her pride if he couldn't handle the sight of her? And face it, she should be able to hide the scars for one night. Covers on and lights off were the way to go.

At the beginning of any relationship with a man she'd liked enough to take a chance on, she'd always told him what had happened and how her body wasn't pretty, but even that hadn't been enough to halt the shocked expressions from appearing when she did expose herself. The front of her body was scarred from here to Africa and back, and, apart from her ex-husband, the men who had seen it had made comments about how beautiful they'd thought she was until the moment they'd set eyes on the rest of her body and slowly over the next days or weeks they'd withdraw and go find a prettier woman to have fun with. Went to show how shallow beauty was, and kind of meant the chances of her finding that special someone to spend her life with were remote. Unless she got over herself.

But it was hard to forget the looks those guys had tried to hide. So now rule number one was get to know the man well, learn to trust him not to hurt her before she finally stripped off for him. That had meant no intimacy in her life since. Yet here she was, thinking otherwise about Finn, which made no sense whatsoever. Maybe she was tired of being sensible.

Now you're sounding like you get down and naked with lots of men.

Which couldn't be further from the truth. There'd been very few over the last couple of years since Hamish walked out of her life three months after they'd returned from Australia's Northern Queensland and the holiday from hell. He'd had an epileptic fit in the sea and she'd raced into the water to get him, even knowing there were stingers about. Saving Hamish had been more important than worrying about getting stung.

The irony was that Hamish was fine once the lifeguards got him back on dry land and pumped the water out of his lungs, while she was in agony when they hauled her out and up onto the beach. They sent her to hospital, where doctors did all they could to help her, but there was little they could do about the stings from the jellyfish except prescribe pain relief. They told her that in most cases the lines left by the stings would disappear after a couple of weeks. Kate was one of the unlucky few to be permanently scarred. The front of her mid torso was not pretty.

She'd already felt insecure and unworthy after

Hamish had struggled to cope with her new look, which had added to her insecurities when she'd started dating again. The scarring wasn't the reason Hamish had left her—apparently he preferred his secretary between the sheets to his wife. It hurt even more that he'd hesitated over leaving her because he'd felt guilty about what had happened that day in Queensland and said it constantly reminded him how it was his fault she'd gone into the water so he'd stayed with her longer than he'd wanted. That had made her feel both angry and rejected.

On one level she knew she was overreacting about how her body looked, but it was hard to ignore and move on. Especially as she'd grown up always hearing how beautiful she was. Occasionally she found herself thinking that it would still be great to have a short fling with a man so good-looking he knocked her socks off. And with Finn not staying around there'd be no repercussions or looking for more fun because he'd be gone in no time at all.

Yeah, sounds perfect.

If only she had the guts to make it happen. If only he didn't see the mess that was her abdomen. If only a lot of things.

When Finn took her elbow to lead the way out amongst the heaving crowd, unprecedented heat shot up her arm. Wow. If one small touch could do that, what would it be like to make out with him? Pulling away, Kate turned to face him, and instantly wished she hadn't. He was smiling at her, looking a little stunned too, as though he'd felt her heat under his hand. What would he think if she ran off the floor and went outside to grab a taxi to take her home—alone? But then she'd never been a coward, other than when it came to her body, so guess that meant she was staying right here, doing the moves.

Forget the moves. Finn's body was a part of the music, almost flowing with the beats. Her throat dried as she watched, mesmerised, forgetting to dance.

'You got lead in your boots?' He grinned.

'Bricks.' Forcing her limbs to move, she did her best to dance, but it was a poor version of her usual style.

'Here, perhaps I can help.' Finn took her hand and spun her around under his arm, spun her back to face him, and kept her hand tight in his. 'That's better.'

It was more than better. Her body had relaxed so suddenly she didn't know if she was coming or going. All she was aware of was Finn. Up so close, his body brought flushes to every area of hers. Just as well he wasn't staying around or she'd be a goner for certain. Tonight was her limit when it came to spending time with him, and the night was young. She spun around again, turned back to him, grinning like an idiot. A very confused idiot. 'Far better.'

'I think so.' Those amazing hips did their thing, still moving in sync with the beat, setting her heart racing at an unbelievable speed.

Looking into Finn's blue eyes and seeing that similar surprise coming back at her, she wondered what was going on. Seemed he hadn't expected to feel attracted to her. Yet he was. It was obvious in the way he kept touching her arms or her hips or her waist, and then abruptly pulling back. She couldn't remember when a man had affected her so sharply—if at all—other than Hamish. Her feet tripped over each other.

Instantly Finn caught her and tucked her in close. 'Careful. Can't have you face-planting on the floor.'

'It wouldn't be a good look.' She wound her arms around him and held tight. Not that she was going to drop to the floor, but any excuse to hold his divine body worked for her. Right now a one-nighter did seem the perfect finish to the evening. And quite likely, if his reactions to her were an indicator that they might be on the same page. Strange how the usual warning lights weren't flashing in her head. Finn was that wonderful?

Oh, yeah.

When the music was stopped so everyone could take a break and top up their drinks, Finn walked with her to the bar and asked, 'Another drink?'

'Thanks.' She'd prefer a kiss but she wasn't rushing. Every moment spent with Finn was the best.

He nodded at the queue at the bar. 'We could be waiting a while.'

'Let's get some fresh air in the meantime.'

He looked at her, his mouth lifting at the corners. 'Good idea.'

The breath she'd been holding leaked across her lips. Phew. They *were* on the same page. Weren't they? She was being quite forward for her. Usually she was the one putting the brakes on when it came to getting close to a man. Said a lot about Finn and how he was affecting her.

Out in the foyer they headed for a quiet, darker corner, now hand in hand. Then Finn was hauling her up against him, his mouth finding hers. Her head spun as she pressed her lips against his. He tasted wonderful, like an aphrodisiac. He *was* an aphrodisiac. His tongue was in her mouth, touching, teasing, turning her on so fast she couldn't keep up. It was as if she'd never had sex before, or hadn't known it could be this wonderful, when they were only kissing for the first time. From top to toes, her body burned with need.

Suddenly Finn set her back, away from his body. His arms dropped to his sides as he took a step away, staring at her as though he'd never seen her before. She stopped breathing, stopped pulsing. What was going on?

'I'm sorry. I can't do this.'

The words blasted through her head like a bullet. 'What?' Rejecting her already? Without knowing anything about her? No way. 'Finn, what's going on?' She thought she was speaking firmly but her voice was shaky.

'It wouldn't be fair on you. There are things about me you don't know.' With that, he turned and strode out of the pub, out of her life. Gone, leaving her aching, shocked that he could do such a thing so abruptly. Almost as if she'd drawn him into something he didn't want, something he'd gone along with to oblige her. But he had said it wouldn't be fair on her.

Damn right it wasn't fair. Despair sliced through her. Once again she'd been rejected, this time for a different reason than usual, one she didn't understand. Worse, it had happened so suddenly.

I'm sorry. I can't do this.

Hamish's words hung in the air, making her shiver. But this time it hadn't been Hamish saying them. That was Finn walking away as though she meant nothing more than a pesky fly. He hadn't said anything else, and she was supposed to accept that? Of course she would, because that was what she'd done in the past. It was who she'd become: a coward when it came to getting close to men.

Kate hugged herself tight. Talk about confusing. She and Finn had danced together and he'd appeared to be happy. He'd been the one to pull her into his arms and start kissing her. Not that it had crossed her mind to back off. She'd wanted his kiss. This was a whole new experience. They'd only started kissing; he hadn't seen the scarring that had driven other men away. But he'd still walked out of the building.

Guess she should be grateful that she wouldn't be exposing her weakness. Except she didn't like that at all. For once she'd actually believed she might've been able to overcome those fears enough to have a wonderful night. Now she'd never know. Finn had gone. It was probably for the best, but it still hurt. She'd wanted him more than she could believe. Which had to be a warning in itself.

Best she head home and take a cold shower, though she'd already cooled off a lot as she watched him walk away. Finn might heat her up fast and have her body craving for him, but he wasn't her type if he could do that so abruptly. If she hadn't seen the shock and disappointment in his eyes she'd have thought he was too confident and sure of himself for her liking. But seeing those expressions made her wonder if there might be a lot more to this man than she could begin to imagine.

He was so damned sexy it was scary. And exciting.

And whatever she'd imagined happening was over before it had even begun. He'd rejected her, as others had before him.

CHAPTER TWO

'OF ALL THE veterinary clinics around Christchurch, why did Finn have to get a position at Darfield Animal Care?' Kate muttered as she drove to work on Monday morning. 'It's not like there aren't other rural vet places in the region.'

Be reasonable.

She'd been working out at Lincoln when they'd met and he wouldn't have a clue that she'd changed jobs. Her chest tightened. She had to get over herself. When Peter had announced to everyone that Finn Anderson was coming on board she'd nearly had a fit. She'd spent the last seven months pushing him out of her head at the moments she felt lonely and in need of some man company, and here he was about to start working at the Darfield clinic.

If she'd known he was taking up a position with the company she'd have turned down the job of Head Domestic Vet in the same clinic and stayed working for the company in their Rolleston branch. No, she wouldn't have, because that would've meant forgoing a pay rise and running the clinic, which she was thrilled to be doing and had been aiming for since she'd first signed up with the company a few months ago. One thing to be thankful for was that Finn would spend a lot of his time away from the clinic working on farms, so they wouldn't be constantly bumping into each other between patients.

But the problem was that she could still remember that sizzling kiss as if it happened yesterday. Hot, steamy, a turn-on like none other she'd experienced in a long time. Now she really did have to file that memory in the trash bin. It was not getting to her again. Not at all. If she started getting hyped up over that kiss when Finn was around, then she had only to remind herself of him saying 'I can't do this' and her head would be back in place. She was not getting into another relationship. Especially not with Finn when they'd be working for the same company because when it fell to dust, which it would because all hers always did, then it would be too awkward.

So she wasn't heading into work early to be in work mode when Finn turned up for the weekly meeting and be introduced to everyone? She wasn't claiming her space before he filled the air with his persona that had her rethinking her determination to remain single?

'Shut up, head.' She turned into the clinic and groaned.

Finn stood beside a ute, glancing around as her car rolled forward, looking too good to be true.

Her hands tightened on the steering wheel. How could one kiss do that? She hadn't been that much into him.

Whatever.

From the moment the boss had told everyone he was joining the company she'd found herself wasting too much time thinking about him. So much for what he'd said as he'd walked away from her. But he had added that it was nothing to do with her. Climbing out of her car, she drew a breath and plastered on a tight smile. 'Hello, Finn.'

'Kate? Are you working here?' He sounded nonplussed, as if he'd been blindsided.

'I changed companies about four months ago.'

'Why?'

'I bought a house out here so it made sense. Being on call is a lot easier now.'

'I can see that. You're happy with the change?'

I was fine until I heard your gravelly voice.

Sexy didn't begin to describe it. Her body suddenly felt hot.

'I am.'

I was until I learned you were starting here.

She got her gear out of the boot and slammed it shut. 'What brought you back home? I thought you intended to be away for some years.'

'My brother and his wife are having a baby and I'd like to be around when he arrives. I've missed my family a lot.' He shrugged. 'Plus the northern winters are horrific.' He sounded quite relaxed. Obviously he hadn't spent the past seven months remembering their kiss.

Unlocking the side door, she said over her shoulder, 'I guess those are as good as any reason.' Had he thought about her at all?

'I think so.' He closed the door behind him and followed her through to her room. 'Do you ever help out with the rural side of things?'

'Very rarely. They have to be really short-staffed for that to happen.'

'So we won't be working together.' Did he have to sound quite so relieved?

Or was she looking for trouble? Quite likely. He'd walked away from her, remember? How could she not remember that whenever she thought about their kiss? He wouldn't want to be all over her now, which should help keep her hormones under control.

'Sometimes you'll have to help out in the clinic. But not often,' Kate added. She should be happy about that, but a little gremlin was teasing her, making her wonder what it would be like to work alongside Finn Anderson.

There was no pretending Finn didn't exist. Nor could she go round giving him the cold shoulder. If that was even possible. So becoming friendly colleagues was the only way this was going to work. Anything deeper would mean trusting him not to hurt her and she didn't do that these days.

Her head spun. Time for a change of subject. 'Go ahead and look around the place.'

'Good idea,' Finn muttered more to himself than Kate as he walked out of her room. He'd already been shown around by Peter, but anything to get away and be able to breathe properly for a moment was good. Of all the people he'd expected to work with, Kate was not one of them. She was the reason he'd applied for this position and not gone knocking on the door at Lincoln Vet Clinic where he used to work.

Hands on hips, Finn shook his head as he stared around the small operating room. So much for avoiding Kate. He'd walked into this eyes wide shut. Then he'd mentioned missing his family. He never, ever, talked about anything personal to anyone. Sure, for most people it wasn't a big deal to admit missing family or friends, but for him that was admitting his heart was involved and his heart was in lockdown. Yet he'd opened his gob and blurted it out to Kate.

For crying out loud, he definitely lost his marbles when he was around her. So much for thinking she hadn't wangled her way into his head that night when he'd kissed her. She'd been lurking in there from the moment he'd walked away without a backward glance. That had been one of the hardest things he'd done in a while.

Imagine if he hadn't left when he did. She'd touched him in such warm, intriguing ways he hadn't known in a long time that he suspected he might never have let her go. Not that he had really. Over the months he'd spent weighing up whether to return home or continue with the career he was carving out in Scotland, he'd told himself it was only because he missed his family and mates, but Kate had been hovering in the background all the time, memories of holding that firm yet giving body against him and those beautiful brown eyes haunting him.

Seeing her get out of her car just now had set his blood heating and his toes tensing, terrifying him to realise how vulnerable he really was. He wasn't going to think about all parts above his feet. So much for believing returning to Canterbury was the right thing to do. After almost four years since breaking up with Amelia, he truly believed he'd finally laid his past relationship to rest and could get on with making the life he wanted, which included keeping control over his heart. He'd paid off his debts and finally begun saving for his own property. Things were on the up, though not when it came to trusting a woman enough to be in his life. Chances of that happening were remote.

But just seeing Kate, already he was in deep trouble. Shaking his head, he concentrated on checking out where everything was kept in the operating room. He was not going to spend his day thinking about Kate. What was the point? Even if she was the most beautiful woman he'd ever set eyes on, plus sexy as all be it, he was not getting involved. He couldn't lose control of his thinking around another woman.

Last time the end result had been appalling, and he doubted it would be great if he tried again. He wouldn't be bankrupted again— because he'd keep a firm grip on things even if the woman he might find wanted to be in control. And he certainly wasn't handing his heart over to be decimated once more. It wasn't going to be straightforward getting on with his future dreams as he'd probably spend all his time looking for problems and even find some that didn't actually exist. He'd become vulnerable, not something he liked to admit.

With Amelia, he'd fallen hard and fast, and

had believed her when she'd sworn she loved him, that she'd do anything to make their life wonderful. He'd believed anything was possible when he was in love with such a wonderful woman. She really had blindsided him, and he'd paid a huge price. Like the fool he'd been, he'd believed her when she'd said she was pregnant despite having already learned how devious she was.

So no falling for Kate allowed. The attraction that flared just talking to her had to back off. *Now.*

What were the chances?

Keeping his distance at work would have its difficult moments but he was sure they could get along fine and not overstep the mark when it came to being workmates, and possibly even friends. Fingers crossed that was how it turned out.

Kate stood at the reception desk looking at the list of patients for the day, wishing she hadn't come in early, trying to ignore the image of Finn as he walked towards her. Even in outdoor clothes suitable for getting down and messy in paddocks as he checked over animals, he looked sexy. But then, some men just did, and this one in particular seemed to make a habit of firing her up when she didn't need it. 'How come you came in early?'

'I was antsy to get started. New job and new people always have me buzzing to get started.'

How come he didn't look as if he was buzzing? 'You've got keys to the place?'

'No, that's why I was hanging around outside, hoping someone would turn up soon. Peter was meant to give me a set on Friday but he was still out on a job when I was coming in to see him, so it never happened.' He looked around the room as he continued.

Avoiding her? Could be he was as uncomfortable about this as she was. But then, why would he be? He hadn't wanted to stay around to see the night out last time they met.

Banging on the front door had her spinning around. A man stood there holding a springer spaniel in his arms, looking frantic. 'Oh, dear.'

Finn beat her to the door and opened it. 'What's happened here?'

Kate called across the room, 'Archie, come in. What's Pippa been up to this time?'

'She's got fish hooks in her paw and mouth. I had to cut the nylon between one in the foot and the other end in her lip as each time she moved she put pressure on them and squealed like she'd been stabbed with a knife.'

Kate shuddered. 'Come through.'

Finn closed the door again and followed them into the surgery. 'Want a hand?' he asked as he helped Archie place Pippa on the table and kept a firm hand on her so she didn't try to leap down to the floor.

Not really, but she wouldn't be churlish. She had to start out how she meant to carry on. 'Sure,' Kate replied. Anyway, it was always better to have an extra pair of hands when the dog might be frightened and snap at her. It was well before opening time so no other staff were here and this sort of situation required two people keeping the dog calm as she worked on the injuries. In fact, they could both do that and get it sorted quicker.

Archie was stroking his pet. 'The boys went fishing last night and didn't put their gear away when they got home. Pippa was snooping in the shed after I let her out for her morning pee and this is what she found. I could wring their necks, the idiots.'

Pippa was known to find all sorts of things that were not good for her, but fish hooks were new. 'Do you know how many hooks are in her mouth?' Kate asked as she pried the dog's mouth open.

'I counted two. Don't know if she's swallowed any though. She was gagging on the way here.'

That didn't sound good. 'I'll need to take an

X-ray of her oesophagus. Then we'll give her a strong sedative while we get those hooks out. If that's okay with you?' she added, knowing Archie never blinked at spending what was necessary when it came to his pets. But she had to ask. It was company policy to outline treatments and expenses. Not that she wouldn't anyway.

'Do whatever you have to.'

'It'll mean keeping your dog here for a few hours,' Finn said before looking to her. 'There're two hooks in this paw as well, one firmly embedded in the pad.'

'Need opening up to remove? You can't cut it and push it through?'

Finn shook his head. 'I think that might cause more harm than an incision.'

'I'll leave you to it, Kate.' Archie looked at Finn. 'Thank you, too.'

'Archie, sorry, I've been remiss.' Because she was struggling to accept Finn now worked here, like it or not. 'This is Finn Anderson. He's just started with us as a rural vet so you'll probably get to see him whenever any of your stock require a vet.'

'Hey, Finn, good to meet you. I breed Charolaise cattle and keep a tight watch over them, which regularly involves you guys.'

'Brilliant. Right up my alley. I've returned

from Scotland where I was involved in looking after Aberdeen herds.'

Archie reached out to shake his hand. 'Sounds good to me. Right, I'm out of here. Give me a bell when Pippa's ready to go home, Kate.'

'Will do.' She'd found two hooks in the dog's mouth, just as Archie had said. The throat looked red and swollen too. 'Right, my girl. I'm going to give you a sedative to keep you calm while we fix this.'

'Starting with an X-ray?'

Finn. For a moment she'd forgotten him, being totally involved in checking over Pippa. 'Yes.' So he didn't entirely rule her mind. Thank goodness for something. Checking the bottle of sedative she'd got from the drug cupboard, she attached a needle and inserted it into the back of Pippa's neck.

Finn was rubbing the dog all the time, keeping her calm.

Kate ignored how that made her feel. 'Hold her still, please.'

Within moments Pippa was sprawled flat on her belly, unaware of anything going on.

'I'll carry her through to the X-ray machine if you show me the way,' he said. 'She's not light.'

'I'm not arguing. She's big for her breed.' The whole litter was, but Pippa was the largest. Before leading the way to the operating room where the X-ray machine was, Kate rubbed the dog's head. She'd known this one from the day she was born as she'd had to do a caesarean when the bitch couldn't push the pups out. 'Through here.'

Finn followed, holding his heavy bundle against his wide chest. It would be lovely to be held there. He was gorgeous. No matter how she felt about them working together she wasn't about to stop thinking that any time soon. Instead she had to learn to ignore the heat that any stray glance generated throughout her sex-starved body.

Flicking the light switch, Kate took a deep breath as she grabbed the machine and rolled it over to the table where Finn was laying Pippa down. His large hand was gentle as he rubbed the dog's flank.

Lucky girl.

Day one, before opening hours at that, and she was already in a dither about the new vet. 'Why did he come here and not go to Lincoln where his mate was?'

The sound of a throat being cleared had her spinning around to come face to face with Finn.

'Because this is my ideal job.'

Her eyes widened and her cheeks were heating up something horrible. 'I didn't mean to say that out loud.'

'So I gathered.' He locked intense eyes on her.

'We're going to have to make this work, Kate. I'm here for the long haul.'

'So am I,' she retorted. Straightening her already tight back, she added, 'We'll be fine.' Then she sighed. This wasn't working. 'It is good to see you again, Finn.' It wasn't quite true. Their abrupt ending last time got in the way of that. On the plus side, maybe she could really get to know him and get over that brief interlude.

'Thanks.'

That was it? Fair enough. He was being sensible. So she'd try and follow suit. Lining up the X-ray plate above Pippa, she asked Finn, 'What about your time with the cattle you were so keen about? Has that made a difference to what you want to do going forward?'

Finn rolled Pippa onto her side with no resistance. The drug had done its job. 'It had got me thinking about what I could do with cattle around here as well as working for Peter. He knows I'm interested in setting up a specialty unit,' he added quickly.

'He's open to anything, is Peter. You didn't want to work somewhere else over that side of the world before you returned home?' Might as well keep the conversation flowing and her mind focused on Pippa's problems.

He shook his head sharply. 'No. It was fun living north of Aberdeen, and the Scots are wonderful people, but I can't see myself living permanently anywhere else but in NZ.'

'Something we have in common.'

'Don't you mean something else? We obviously both enjoy working with animals.'

She relaxed a little, even managed to smile. 'Can't argue with that. Right, stand back.' She waited until he'd moved away from the table before pressing the button to take the X-ray. Within moments she had the answer to whether they'd have to operate. 'She didn't swallow any hooks.'

'That's a relief.'

'It certainly is. I think the gagging is because of a small piece of bone in the oesophagus, which'll slowly make its way through her system.' Collecting a clipper to cut through the metal hooks and a kit to suture the wounds, she asked, 'You want to deal with the paw while I deal with her mouth?'

'More than happy to.'

'There's a largish hole in the back of the tongue where one hook's gone through. Could be the one that was pulled when Pippa tried to stand on her foot.'

'Need stitching?'

'Hopefully not. It would be better to let it heal naturally as the hard ends of the thread will aggravate her more than the wound. I'll give Archie antibiotics and pain reducers to feed her over the next few days.'

The room was quiet for a while as they both worked on fixing Pippa.

When Kate stepped back from the table, she rubbed her lower back. She'd never got used to bending over a table while working on an animal. 'Thanks for your help.'

'Glad I was here.'

The door opened and Peter, the owner and overall boss, walked in. 'Morning, you two. I see you're already hard at work.'

'Archie turned up at the door with Pippa in his arms. She'd managed to get hold of some fish hooks.' Kate began clearing away the needles and thread.

'Where do I put her?' Finn asked.

'In the next room.' She opened a door and headed for one of the cages. 'This is our recovery room.' She watched as he knelt down and slid Pippa inside the cage so carefully it almost brought tears to her eyes. Bet he was just as gentle with the humans in his life. A big softie on the inside, not quite as much outwardly. He hadn't been with her. Not if the way he'd walked away from her that night was anything to go by after saying he had issues he was dealing with.

She had to admit it had been for the best. If they had gone further and become intimate, she would not have wanted to see his eyes widen with shock and hear derogatory words spill from that divine mouth if he saw her scars. It was hard to take from anyone, but for some inexplicable reason she thought it might've been even worse coming from Finn.

'There you go, Pippa.' Finn stood up and turned to Peter. 'Great way to start the day.'

'You were obviously early. Couldn't sleep for the excitement of meeting everyone?' Peter grinned.

'Absolutely.'

'Well, you've met Kate, and worked with her already, so that's a start.'

'I agree,' Finn said, not mentioning the fact they'd already met.

'I'm going to put the coffee on shortly if either of you want one,' Kate told them as she dumped the wipes she'd used to clean the table.

'Count me in for coffee, unless Peter has other ideas,' Finn replied. 'I haven't had my caffeine fix yet.'

'Give me five.' She turned away from those intense sky-blue eyes and focused on the computer screen to enter Pippa's details and email Archie a message saying his dog was fine and would be good to go home in a few hours.

'Jack's surgery's been cancelled,' Di, the vet nurse, called through another door leading into

Reception. Seemed everyone was turning up for work now.

Kate went through to see her. 'That must mean he's healing nicely.'

'His owner says his foot's looking good and he's running around like crazy once more. You must've removed the seed causing all the trouble the other day despite not being certain about it.'

'Hopefully that's the case. Surgery on his paw would've made life difficult for a few days for him and his owners.' Grass seeds between dogs' toes were a continuous problem, especially for those with long hair on their paws.

'Shall I make the coffee while you do what you have to out here?' Finn asked from behind her.

Turning around, she saw him press his lips together firmly. Did she rattle him as much as he did her? She drew a breath. This had to stop. If she just acted naturally these feelings of annoyance that he was on her patch would eventually subside. 'White with one,' she answered. It wasn't necessary he make the coffee but he'd offered and she'd accept. First step towards plan 'friendly'. Yes, she'd changed it from colleagues to friendly workmates already.

Ten minutes later, when she entered the tea-room, she struggled to dampen the heat filling her. Finn was sitting at the far end of the room and there were two mugs of coffee on the table in front of him, as well as an empty chair next to his. The last place she wanted to sit when the sparks were going off inside her. She remained on her feet and reached for the closest mug. 'Thanks.'

'Any time.'

'Have you met any of the others yet?'

'Only Di and Mark.' Mark was another vet.

'Let me fix that.' Kate went out to see who was around and brought them through to the tearoom, where she introduced everyone. Within a short time everyone had joined them, and Finn was welcomed like a long-lost friend. They had been down one rural vet since Gavin had been knocked down by a bull he was supposed to be vaccinating. It had put pressure on everyone as the hierarchy had waited until they knew if he'd return to rural veterinary work or settle for domestic duties.

'I'm not going to remember everyone's names straight up.' Finn chuckled as he drank his coffee. 'You'll all have to be patient with me for a while.'

Peter strolled into the room. 'Since everyone's here I'll grab a few minutes of your time before we get on with the day, though I'm sure those of you who have to work outside will want me to drag this out.' The heavy clouds were now bucketing rain and not looking like stopping any time soon.

There were pluses to working inside the clinic, Kate mused as she focused on Peter and not Finn.

'First of all, welcome to Canterbury Vets and especially the Darfield clinic, Finn. We're glad to have you on board. Any questions?'

Finn shook his head. 'Not so far. I'm pleased to be here and look forward to working with everyone.'

Even her? Kate sipped coffee and stared at the tabletop. So far he'd been friendly enough. Working together with Pippa had gone well and been no different from working with any other vet in the practice.

'We've been asked to have a tent once more at the local school pet fair in April, where we can discuss various matters with pet owners. As we know from the past, we'll get kids bringing in their dogs, cats and rabbits for us to see and check over. It's all good fun and we sell loads of toys.' Peter looked at Finn. 'It's a community event, and we usually get a few new customers out of it.'

'I'm happy to start putting lists together of what we'll need and who wants to volunteer for the day,' Kate said.

Peter nodded. 'Thanks, Kate. The lists are still

there from last year but could do with some up-dating.'

'Anything I can do to help?' Finn asked.

'You can work with Kate from the rural perspective,' Peter suggested. 'Some youngsters bring along their pet calves. Mark, you look like you want to say something.'

Kate scowled. Thanks, Peter, she thought, but he was only getting things sorted for the day.

Mark said, 'Count me in too. It's actually fun as a vet being out there amongst the locals and not behind a table with a sick animal and worried owner.'

Within minutes Kate had a list of volunteers and everyone was getting up to start their day. 'That was easy,' she said to the room in general.

'We all know you're a pushover when it comes to handing out the tricky jobs.' Mark laughed.

She laughed back at him. 'For that you get to do the poop collections.'

'Knew I should've kept my mouth shut.' Mark headed out of the door.

Turning to put her mug in the dishwasher, Kate found Finn watching her with an amused expression.

'What?'

'Where did you come up with that idea from?'

'Poop collections? They're for real.'

'I did not come down in the last rain shower.'

How that smile got to her, made her hot in places
best not thought about right now. 'We're going to
be in a tent, not wandering around the grounds
with animals.'

'Damn, then I'll have to find another ghastly
job for Mark.'

Di appeared at the door. 'Vicki's here with
Frankie, Kate. She's due an allergy shot.'

'Vicki or Frankie?' she quipped, then shook
her head to clear Finn out of it. 'Coming.' She
needed to do some serious work on not being
distracted whenever he was near. 'See you later,'
she said as she stepped around him.

'I'll take a look at Pippa while I'm waiting
for Peter.'

Peter had taken a phone call and gone to his
office.

'If that's all right with you?' Finn asked, as
though suddenly realising he might be treading
in her domain.

'Go for it. Let me know if anything's changed.'
Friendly co-workers, right?

'All's good with Pippa. She's awake and alert,
but not moving much,' Finn told Kate when she'd
finished with the miniature schnauzer named
Frankie.

'So she's not licking her paw. That's good.'
Kate stood up from the computer. 'Are you

working out in the fields today? Or is it all about orientation?'

'I'm heading out to Kirwee once Peter's gone through some data with me and handed over a set of keys. I've got a Highlander bull to see. He's got suspected bovine virus diarrhoea. Apparently not the first on this particular farm, and there's likely to be more, since the farmer was slow in separating him from the herd.'

Kate winced. 'Now I remember why I prefer working with domestic animals. Antsy bulls are not my thing.' The animal would be moody because of the symptoms. 'I hope you're very careful around this one.'

'I'm very cautious around all bulls, antsy or not. Especially Highlanders with their huge horns poking out sideways and able to impale me in an instant just by turning their head to see what I'm doing.' It was one thing he did fear. Those horns were evil.

'Glad to hear it. I've heard a couple of stories of vets and farmers being injured or worse by horns.'

'Haven't we all? I'll let you get on with your patients and go see what Peter's got to show me. Catch up some time during the day.' He closed the door behind him, denying the fact he'd said that. He'd meant to say maybe they'd bump into each other over the week, not catch up as though they'd sit down and have a yarn, but it hadn't come out like that. No wonder her beautiful fudge eyes had widened. He could drown in those eyes. So big and warm, even when she was keeping her distance.

Oh, yes, he knew she'd been brassed off in the tearoom. The annoyance in her eyes had been a dead giveaway. He hadn't done it deliberately. It had been a thoughtless move and to have shoved her coffee across the table to another spot would've suggested he was affected by her. Something he wasn't letting on. They had to get along. It might take some practice on his part, but he'd make sure they did. For everyone's sake. Especially his.

CHAPTER THREE

'DAMN AND BLAST,' Kate muttered when she headed outside the clinic to go home at the end of the Friday evening session. She was tired, her back ached from too many operations earlier in the day, and now her car had a flat tyre. 'Just what I need.'

Tossing her bag on the front seat, she popped the boot and cleared the assorted boxes and bags of gear off the spare tyre. 'Why do I carry around so much junk?' Most of it was there for times when she was required to help an injured animal outside the clinic, but at moments like this she wished she were less OTT about having absolutely everything she might need, and then some.

The tyre was heavy to lift out of the well. Leaning it against the back of the car, she hunted around for the jack and spanner, and sighed with relief when she found them in the bottom of the well. This shouldn't take too long, she thought. It wasn't the first tyre she'd ever changed.

'Here, I'll give you a hand.' Finn was striding across from his ute.

She hadn't heard him pull in. That was a good sign, as it meant he didn't feature in her mind all the time. 'I've got this.'

'Don't be stubborn, Kate. I'm not leaving, so you might as well step aside and let me do the job.'

'And if I don't?' Why was she being so stubborn? Because Finn was right; that was exactly what she was doing. If it had been Peter or Mark she wouldn't have refused the offer.

'I'm being a gentleman. Make the most of it.' His smile was flippant but his eyes were sincere.

'It doesn't happen often?' she asked, stepping aside because the sooner the job was done, the sooner she could head home, and put distance between them.

'I do my best.' Kneeling down, he placed the jack under the axle, then stood to use his foot to operate the lever.

Another retort came to mind, but as she looked at Finn her heart clenched and she kept it to herself. He was being kind, and didn't deserve any grief because she had issues with men. Throw in the fact that he wound her up fast just by being here and she was all over the place with knowing what to do about her reactions to him. 'Thank you for doing this.'

'It's all right. I'm sure you'd have it under control in no time but there's no way I could've walked away.'

'I know.' The thing was, she truly did. She mightn't have had much to do with him all week but it came through loud and clear he was a gentleman—when he wasn't walking away from a kiss and the sensuous sensations that had caused. Of course, he might've done that because he *was* a gentleman and didn't want to take advantage of her. Not that he had been because she'd been ready for some fun, but he wouldn't necessarily know that. 'What brought you here at this hour? I'd have thought you'd be long gone.' It was the end of the week and anyone not needed was well and truly gone.

'I need to top up with some drugs for a farm visit I've got lined up in the morning.'

Nothing unusual in that. 'How's your first week been?'

'Brilliant. There're a lot of farms on the books to keep me busy, and so far the farmers I've met have been friendly and ready to take advice.' The wheel was off and Finn was lining up the spare onto the studs. 'Very similar to where I worked at in Scotland.'

'You don't sound like you're missing that place.'

'I haven't been back in Canterbury long yet,

so no. But I doubt I'll miss more than a couple of friends. Where I was is a beautiful part of Scotland, but not the sort of place where I'd want to live for ever. Too bleak and cold. Summer lasts weeks, not months. At least here we know when it snows that there will be extremely hot temperatures in the summer to make up for it.'

'You into skiing by any chance?' Mountains ran down the centre of the South Island and there were ski fields not far from Darfield.

'I did some when I was growing up, and got more into it in Scotland. I intend to keep on with it now that I'm back, though winter's a way off right now.' He suddenly looked annoyed, but she had no idea why. The tyre was on and he was fastening the bolts so it couldn't be because there was a problem there.

'Not a lot of snow to be found at the moment.' She'd love to see those long legs swishing down the mountainside.

You wouldn't be with him.

There was a point.

'What drugs do you want? I can get them while you finish up.'

'Thanks.'

Why hadn't she thought about it sooner instead of hanging around watching Finn? The answer was in the question really. He was quite an eyeful. 'What do you need?' she asked sharply.

After he told her what he wanted, he stood up and surprised her. 'Feel like going to the local for a drink? I haven't got any reason to rush home and thought it would be nice to have a yarn with someone I know.'

So he wasn't desperate to spend time with her, only in need of some company. Not as settled in yet as he made out to be? Her instinct was to decline but she hesitated. She did understand he was new to the area and it couldn't hurt to be friendly. Mightn't hurt, but she'd be a mess by the time she got home if she did go. It was part of doing the friendly thing, not the hot, sexy, 'I want your body' one. And one drink wouldn't hurt. Hopefully she could manage that without getting in a bigger dither over him.

'Which pub are you thinking of?'

'That one around the corner from here. The Hunters' Retreat?'

'Yep, that's it. Okay, let's do it.' She turned for the door leading inside. 'I'll be back in a minute with those meds.'

After I've checked my make-up and tidied my hair.

'No rush. This is all but done. I'll put the damaged tyre in the back. You need to get it repaired asap in case it happens again.'

'There's a tyre shop along the road. I'll drop it in tomorrow morning.' She headed inside without a backward glance, which was hard because all she wanted to do was turn around and drink in the sight of Finn. Where had that come from when she'd been comfortable and not distracted—much—while talking about skiing? He went and suggested they go to the pub together and suddenly she was melting on the inside. It was going to need to be an ice-cold drink to cool her down.

Her hair was in a lopsided, messy ponytail. Tugging the band off, she brushed the knots into something tidier. A girl had to look her best when she was with a jaw-dropping, good-looking man. Except when at work. As for her make-up, it wasn't too bad and she didn't want to look as if she was going all out to impress him. But it was so tempting. Her lipstick was in her hand before she thought about it. Okay, what the heck? It was normal to put some on whenever she was going anywhere unless it was to help a ewe give birth to a lamb.

'Shall we walk?' Finn asked when she rejoined him and handed over the drugs he'd requested.

'Why not?' It would be good to get some fresh air after a day inside. It might also go some way to helping her cool down. 'It's barely five hundred metres. Besides, parking there's often a nightmare on Friday nights. It is the locals' favourite pub.'

'So I heard.'

Walking beside Finn didn't quite cool anything. His arm had a habit of rubbing against her shoulder whenever she dodged an uneven patch on the footpath. Not many of them but enough to make her even more aware of her colleague. Yes, keep thinking about Finn like that and hopefully she'd get over this unusual reaction. Think about the scars and that would certainly put everything into perspective.

'Are you living in the township or further afield?' he asked.

'I bought an older house with a half-acre section on the back street about a year ago. I'm supposed to be doing up the house but there's never much spare time. One day I'll get it done.' When the mortgage was a little less eye-watering she'd put in a new kitchen and bathroom. Since her housemate had moved away there was less spare money to spend. She needed to get someone else to rent the spare room. 'I'm a beginner when it comes to painting.'

'Can't say I've done a lot either, though my ex and I were starting to do up the house we bought in Wellington,' Finn told her.

'So like mine, not a new house?' An ex, eh? Another thing they had in common.

'A nineteen-twenties bungalow in Karori. It was a cold hole as they didn't know about insulation back in the days when it was built. Winters were hell, but nowhere near as bad as Scotland.'

Kate shivered despite the warmth. 'I hate the cold, which is why the first thing I replaced when I moved into the house was the fireplace. It was in rough condition. I probably burnt more firewood last winter than everyone else around here put together.'

'Got a local farmer on hand with lots of trees to fell, by any chance?' Finn laughed.

His laugh was warm and friendly, and added to the heat coursing through her. 'One or two.' He could move into her house for winter and she wouldn't need any firewood. Except she'd then need a lock and key on her hormones.

He took her elbow as they reached the pub door. 'It's certainly busy.'

It would be rude to pull away when his hand felt good against her skin. It really had been a while since she'd enjoyed the simple touch of a man. So much for thinking she didn't need one in her life, if this was how she reacted to Finn. 'Where are you living?'

Closing the door behind them, he took her elbow again and led them to a table with bar stools. 'I'm temporarily renting a flat in West Melton. What would you like to drink?'

In other words, ask no more. 'G and T, thanks.'

The scowl that had been growing disappeared. 'Be right back.'

What was wrong with asking where he was living? It wasn't a big deal, surely? But then she was still getting to know him and he often didn't seem to like talking about himself. Which could make for a quiet evening, she mused, because she liked getting to know people, even when it was this man.

'Hi, Kate.' Peter appeared beside her. 'I see you're with Finn. That's good. He needs to get to know all of us so he'll feel settled and not think of leaving.'

'He only started this week.'

'I know, but I'd hate to lose him. He's darned good at what he does and getting new vets isn't easy these days.'

Quite a few were going offshore once they'd qualified and not all were returning home in a hurry, if at all. 'I don't think Finn has any intention of moving away. He's home for family.' She glanced over at him coming their way, then back at Peter.

'Good.' Peter's face broke into a smile. 'Finn, good to see you out and about.'

'Hey, Peter. Can I get you a drink?' Finn placed a glass in front of her.

'Thanks, but if I don't head home my missus

will have something to say about cooking dinner being a waste of time. See you both next week.'

'Bye.' Kate turned to Finn. 'Sheree, Peter's wife, is a hard case. She'd never make him go without his meal, but she does let him know what she thinks whenever he's late. When they were young and raising their three kids, she was a vet nurse and running the home, while Peter was doing extra papers and setting up his own practice. I don't think it was easy for either of them.'

'I bet it wasn't.'

'You haven't thought of starting your own practice?' With his experience in Scotland, it would make sense.

Finn all but poured beer down his throat before putting the glass back on the table heavily. 'I had one once. Before I left for Britain. It was in Wellington, not rural. I had to close it down.' Definitely not happy talking about his past.

There was a lot to Finn she had no idea about, but she got his reaction in bucketloads because she was reluctant to talk about her past too. Especially her trust issues. Did he have those too? 'I didn't mean to upset you.'

'I guess you won't be the only person at the practice to ask me, merely the first.'

'Everyone we work with is genuinely nice and they'll want to get to know you. It's not like they want to learn some gossip to spread around. If they did, they'd have been on the Internet by now.'

Finn's eyes darkened, and his nod was abrupt. 'Don't I know it.' More beer went down his throat, then he sighed heavily. 'I was engaged to be married at the time. To an accountant. She bankrupted us.' His words were abrupt and there was a load of hurt in his face.

Kate wished she could reach out and take his hand in hers, hold him tight, but she sensed he wouldn't appreciate that at all. Nor would it help her determination to keep her distance. 'I bet that's still a bitter pill to swallow.'

His eyes weren't so sky-blue now, more a dark, gloomy shade. 'Very.'

She'd also bet he wouldn't have a lot of trust these days when it came to women. What his ex had done would have been devastating, not only to his dreams of owning his own business, but more than that, his heart must've been shattered. Her chest tightened. She was completely in sync with him on that one. 'I am really sorry for overstepping the line.'

'You weren't to know.'

'Of course not.'

His smile was tight. 'Obviously no one mentioned it at work in Lincoln after the party.'

Kate shook her head. 'Not at all.' She opted

to grin and hopefully lift his mood, along with hers. 'Everyone was so stoked at how well the party went, they didn't talk about anything else for a week.'

Sipping his beer, Finn slowly relaxed and finally gave her a genuine smile. 'Thanks for not making a big deal out of it. It's in the past and I'm moving on, setting up a new life, which I hope will include a specialty business.'

'Going to Britain was to put distance between you and your ex?'

'That and to earn some decent money so I could rectify some of the debts.'

Wow. That said a lot about the man. Declared bankrupts weren't obliged to pay back money owed to creditors. They couldn't obtain a loan for a set period of time either. It must've been a few years back when Finn lost everything if he was legally able to start a new business now, but then he hadn't said he was doing that yet. Of course, he probably didn't have the funds either.

'You're too quiet,' he growled. Worried about what she might be thinking?

'And you don't like that. Fair enough. I am getting my head around what you've told me, but, rest assured, I'm not making a big deal out of it. From the little I've seen of you this week, I can't imagine you'll be sitting still and not making a successful future for yourself.' Picking up her glass, she tapped it against his. 'Here's to you.'

Finn tapped back. 'Thanks, Kate.' He looked around for a long moment, as if deciding something. Once more he surprised her. 'Feel like something to eat? I'm starving.'

'Me too. I'll have fish and chips.' So much for one drink and going home. She still should do that but right now she felt comfortable with Finn. She wanted to offer to get the meals but instantly thought he'd probably think she was being sympathetic about how he'd lost his money, so she kept quiet on that score. Anyway, for all she knew he might be floating in money by now.

'Blue cod or snapper?'

'Definitely cod.'

'You're my kind of woman.' His smile slipped. 'I mean—'

This time she did grab his hand for a brief moment, and instantly felt a flare of heat. Letting go fast, she said in a shaky voice, 'If you'd said you were having hoki I'd have walked out the door.' Not really, but the air between them had suddenly got heavy again and needed lightening. He also needed to see he could trust her to have some time out together without getting deep and worrisome.

'Hi, Kate. Finn. Thought I'd let you know Pippa's doing fine. No one would believe she'd got those hooks in her foot on Monday.' Archie stood between them. 'Thank you both so much.'

Kate laughed to herself. There was never a lot of privacy at this pub. Just as well she'd removed her hand from Finn's before Archie had appeared.

'That's the best news,' Finn told him. 'How did the boys take what had happened?'

'They got a bollocking, but to be fair they were both very remorseful. It won't happen again.'

'Good to hear,' Kate added her bit. She'd heard from one of the vet nurses that Pippa was doing well with no side effects. 'Let's hope we don't see you for a while.'

Archie shrugged. 'What are the chances?' He turned to Finn. 'We've got four dogs, two cats and the herd of cattle I told you about. Something's always happening to one of my animals.'

'To be expected when you've got that many.' Finn was looking more relaxed by the minute.

'I'll leave you two to it and get home. Thanks again,' he said before heading away.

'The good side to being a vet,' Finn said. 'I'll go order the food.'

Kate watched him moving through the crowded tables, a head above nearly everyone. His dark blond hair was a mess and fell over the edge of his shirt collar. His shoulders were firm, not tight as they'd been when he'd mentioned his past. The back view was good, and when there was a gap in the crowd and she could see his taut butt the view got even better. That was one sexy rear. A ten out of ten.

Quickly swallowing a big mouthful of gin and tonic that wasn't as cold as it had first been, she looked away, trying to find something or someone to focus on until the heat in her veins backed off. It was a fail. There were no interesting distractions. But recalling that night and those words, 'I can't do this', might do the trick. Those words had resonated in her mind time and again whenever she thought about Finn. Now that they were working together she needed to keep his statement foremost in her mind as there was no way they were going to be more than friends.

No man she'd liked enough to get close to had wanted a bar of her once they'd seen the damage done to her skin, and she particularly did not want that happening with Finn. Why was she attracted to such shallow men? Just because she'd been born with good facial looks it didn't mean she was perfect all over, inside and out. Nobody was.

Not saying Finn was shallow from what she'd seen so far though. In fact, when she wasn't being careful, he had her thinking the impossible—getting up close and indecent with him. But recalling how he'd repeated Hamish's words 'I can't do this' did pull the brakes on a little. Add in that he had a lot of baggage and she needed to be even more cautious. He wasn't going to accept her so easily, if he even wanted more from her. Nor could she blame him. She was still getting over Hamish leaving her and he hadn't done half of what Finn's fiancée did to him.

Finn placed napkins and salt and pepper shakers on the table. 'Shouldn't be too far away. The kitchen's humming.'

'They have a good rep for their food.'

'What were you thinking about?' he asked. 'You appeared to be miles away.'

Getting way ahead of myself when I'm not sure what I want.

'Thinking how my two fur babies will be curled up on my bed waiting for me to get home and light the fire.'

'I'm picking dogs, not cats.'

'Bang on. My neighbour's daughter looks after them when I'm late home, which is a big help. It also gives her some money to buy the things teenagers can't seem to do without.'

'I heard there's a pet day care in town. It's amazing how many people have dogs these days and go that extra distance to make sure they're looked after when they're at work.'

He wasn't suggesting she shouldn't leave her boys at home, was he? 'It's a small centre as most people have large properties and their pets are fenced in so they can wander around all day without getting into trouble. Mine are well past that puppy stage where everything is an adventure so I have no concerns about leaving them at home. Charlotte takes them for a walk after school, and feeds them if I'm late.'

'You'd be the last person I'd expect not to have all the bases covered. You're a vet and a caring woman.' He drained his beer. 'Want another drink?'

It wasn't far to walk home. She could indulge for once. 'Yes, thanks. How about I get them?'

He shook his head. 'Tonight's my turn. You can offer some other time.'

She gave him a smile. 'Offer? Not pay?' He really was great to be with when she wasn't coming up with every reason in the book to hold him at arm's length, or jump his bones.

'You read me too easily.' Picking up the glasses, he headed back to the bar.

And she watched him again. Should've asked for a double serve of ice, she conceded as her skin warmed. He'd sounded certain when he'd said she was a caring woman. Wow. He was getting to her in more ways than the one where her body overheated.

Should've gone home while she could without looking silly.

CHAPTER FOUR

'I'LL DRIVE YOU HOME,' Finn told Kate when they were ready to leave the pub. She had said she'd walk but there was no way he'd let her now darkness had fallen. He'd only had two beers, with fish and chips thrown in, so he was good to drive.

'Cheers. That'd be great.'

Too easy. With this woman he was always looking for the problems, not the straightforward acceptance that they were working partners. It was proving difficult to put her out of his mind. Even at work, when they were busy with animals and their sometimes distressed owners, she slipped into his head. Like unfinished business that needed dealing with. But that couldn't be right. Finding an ideal woman for his future wasn't part of his game plan.

'Let's go.' Shoving his hand in his pocket to prevent himself taking her arm because that would seem too keen, he headed for the door and held it open while she stepped past him, teasing his nostrils with the scent of spring flowers.

Kate flicked her hair back from her face. 'The temperature's barely dropped a degree since we got here.'

'Is your house cool in summer?'

'It gets a bit stuffy if I don't leave windows open.'

'That's safe to do?'

'With the dogs roaming the section it is.' There was a softness in her voice whenever she mentioned her pets.

'Do they come first in your household?'

'First, second, and third. I love them to bits. They came from a couple out this way who were moving into a retirement village and felt it was unfair to keep them in such a small space after living on a farm. I had been thinking about getting Labrador puppies but the time needed for training seemed daunting when I've already got a lot on.' A light laugh fell between them. "Besides, I'd be too soft with them, and they'd never have grown up into sensible dogs.'

He believed her. 'How old are the two you've got?'

'Rusty's four and Sam's three.'

A phone rang. It wasn't his call sound.

Kate pulled hers from the bag slung over her shoulder. 'Charlotte? What's up?'

Finn found himself moving quicker to keep up with her.

'How did that happen? I thought I'd shut the gate this morning. Charlotte, it's not your fault, okay? I'm on my way. I'll be five minutes, no more.' She gripped her phone at her side. 'Rusty's hurt himself. Charlotte says his front leg is at an odd angle and he howls every time he moves.'

This time Finn didn't hesitate to take her hand to keep Kate steady as they raced back to the clinic, where he had his vehicle unlocked in an instant. 'Which way?' he asked as he turned the ignition on.

'Left, then second right. The little brat jumped the fence and got his leg caught in the wires. Charlotte thinks it was injured when he fell further. He was swinging when she found him.' Kate brushed the back of her hand over her face. 'So much for being a sensible, serious vet. This is doing my head in. What if—?'

Finn cut her off. 'Don't go there. Wait until we've assessed the injury.' He'd be there to support her, and do whatever was required for the dog too. Which probably meant taking him back to the clinic.

'We? Thank you.'

His heart sank. 'You didn't think I'd help you?'

'Finn, I'm not thinking straight. Of course I didn't think that.'

The beating in his chest returned to normal. 'You're a stressed mum,' he said lightly. Imagine how she'd be if this had happened to a child of hers. The sort of mother any kid would be lucky to have. And any dog, he admitted with a wry smile.

'That drive on your right. Charlotte's opened the gate for us.'

Lights were on inside the house. The girl was probably as stressed as Kate. 'Want me to bring my gear in?' Who knew what they might need to make Rusty comfortable?

'Yes. I've got a kit in the laundry but you'll know your way around yours.' She was out of the car, running up the steps to the front door.

Bag in hand, he followed the voices inside. Kate was kneeling by a couch where a cocker spaniel lay, panting fast. A continuous low moan was audible, making Finn want to touch Kate on the back so she'd know she wasn't alone. Instead he knelt beside her, and said to the girl hovering over the couch with tears spilling down her face, 'Hi, Charlotte. I'm Finn, also a vet. How did you get Rusty inside?' He began feeling the twisted leg while keeping an eye on the dog in case he reacted badly to the touch.

'He hopped in very slowly, crying all the time.'

Kate put her hand on the dog's head, and rubbed his back with her other hand. 'That's the boy. Easy, easy.'

'I don't think the leg's broken. I suspect a torn ligament,' Finn said. 'We need to take him for an X-ray. I don't want to do too much checking out until he's sedated and best I do that at the clinic.'

'Agreed,' Kate said, still stroking her boy. 'We're probably going to have to do surgery, aren't we?' Asking that showed how upset she was. She knew the answer.

Touching her shoulder, he nodded. 'I'll do it if it's necessary.'

'Thanks.'

No argument whatsoever. That had to be a plus. He'd have thought Kate would insist on taking care of her beloved pet. There was still lots to learn about her. 'What about your other dog?'

'I'll take Sam home with me,' Charlotte answered before Kate had a chance. 'He's used to our place.'

'He'll be restless with Rusty not there,' Kate pointed out.

'I know, but he can sleep on my bed.' Charlotte finally smiled.

'Your mother will not be pleased.'

'Tough.' Charlotte grinned, then turned serious. 'Will Rusty be all right? It wasn't my fault.

A kid was taking his puppy down the road and Rusty went spare.'

'That's not like him.' Charlotte stood up and reached for the girl, wrapped her in a hug. 'Stop blaming yourself. I know you'd have been looking out for him.'

Opening his kit, Finn found the vial for pain relief and attached it to a needle. 'Here we go, Rusty. Just a quick jab to make you comfortable on the short trip to the clinic.' The needle slid into the flesh on the back of the dog's neck and Finn pressed down on the syringe. 'There, all done.' Already the dog was quietening down.

Kate gave him a tight, heart-wrenching smile. 'I definitely owe you a drink and dinner now. Thank you for helping.'

He lifted Rusty into his arms. 'Will you stop saying that? You'd be doing the same if this was the other way round.'

'True.'

Once the dog was loaded onto the back seat of his ute and Kate had locked up after Charlotte had left with Sam, they were on their way, Kate sitting in the back, rubbing her pet's head.

'You're a big softie,' Finn told her.

'I know. It's bad enough when this happens to someone else's dog, but I feel sick when it's mine. Have you got any pets?'

'Not yet. There hasn't been a lot of time since

I returned home, what with finding somewhere to live and getting other things sorted out.' Like talking to his lawyer about a mortgage now he was almost free to get one again, and tying up everything he owned so that if he ever made the mistake of falling in love with the wrong person he'd at least still have his assets. Not that they were the most important of everything he'd lost with Amelia.

A glance in the rear-view mirror brought on a rare longing for a woman to go home to at the end of the day, to sit down and relax over a meal and share their days with. When he wasn't being too self-protective he could admit to how much he missed having that special someone in his life. Plus the dreams for the future that went along with that. Family.

He shivered. This was plain crazy for him to be thinking like that. He wasn't going there at the moment when it appeared that Kate had no one to share those things with either. She hadn't phoned anyone since getting the call from Charlotte so he'd stepped up. Seeing her distress about her dog was sad. But he wouldn't be there for her all the time. He was not going down that route no matter how much he was beginning to like her.

'Have you got family around here?'

'Mum and Dad recently moved to a new subdivision in Lincoln, which is a huge downsize for them after spending the last twenty-two years on fifty acres out near here in Kirwee. They thought it was time to go, but I'm not so sure. Dad's always trying to find things to do and now mows lawns for half the people in their street.'

'Sounds like a man with a big heart.' Was that where Kate got hers from?

'He is. My brothers have moved away. One's a doctor in Taupo, and the other's a civil engineer working in Western Australia.'

'Bet you miss them.'

'I do. Big time.'

'I felt that way about my brother, and Mum and Dad, when I was in Scotland.' They were the main reason behind why he'd returned home ahead of time, hoping he was ready to get on with making a new life on old turf. The nagging memory of kissing Kate had been a teaser, not a solid reason to come back. Though he had thought about her as though he'd missed a wonderful opportunity by walking away from that kiss; an opportunity he was still reluctant to risk everything on.

But the fact he'd never forgotten Kate told him he wasn't as in control of his feelings as he'd like to believe. Throw in the fact he knew he'd done all he could while away to put Amelia behind him, and the time had definitely arrived to move forward.

Another glance in the mirror at the beautiful woman in the back. No. No matter what happened between them, he wasn't going so far as to involve his heart. That would be a serious move and there was a lot to learn about Kate before he even considered giving in to the intense sensations of longing she caused. She might be creating havoc in his head and body, but that was as far as she was going. He was not looking to tie the knot with another woman. Never.

'Have you ever been in a permanent relationship? Or married?'

'I'm divorced.' She looked up at him as if to ask where that came from, then she glanced back at Rusty. 'I found the man of my dreams and got married six years ago. All was going great, or so I thought. Then we went away on holiday to Port Douglas for what I believed was to be a lovers' retreat, only Hamish had apparently fallen out of love but was giving it one last shot. Three months later we split up. End of everything.' Kate hadn't looked up from Rusty while telling him that.

Finn felt for her. What she'd told him was a bland outline with loads of pain behind the words. He understood the need to play it down, not drag sympathy out of others. It didn't get you anywhere and made you feel worse. 'Life's a bitch,' he admitted.

'Sure can be.'

He turned into the clinic parking yard and the automatic lighting came on.

Behind him, Kate was talking to her pet in a velvet voice that tickled Finn's skin and had him questioning himself about remaining aloof, especially now he knew she'd been hurt. He thought he wanted to make her feel better, and himself along the way, which went against everything he believed would be right for him. Scary to say the least.

'Here we go, my boy.' Kate opened the door and began helping the dog out.

'I'll open up and turn some lights on inside.' He headed for the main entrance, focusing on what he had to do for the dog, and not himself. Turning around, he hesitated when he saw Kate leaning over, holding Rusty's collar as she carefully led him towards the clinic. He was wobbly on his feet, but making slow progress. 'Do you want me to carry him?'

'No, we'll be slow but we'll get there. He's not moaning so the painkillers are working.'

Finn did lift the dog onto the X-ray table. He wasn't letting Kate struggle with the weight and difficulty of picking up an injured animal. Rusty wasn't huge but neither was he light. 'There we go. You want me to handle everything?' Kate had said yes earlier but he wanted to be certain and not cause any awkwardness between them. He also really wanted to do this for Kate. He didn't have an answer as to why, other than he liked her and she was hurting over her pet, like any client.

'Go for it. I'd only start seeing things that probably aren't there.' Her smile was tight. A little shudder touched Kate. 'Is this what parents go through every time their child hurts themselves? It must be hard on them.' Her face filled with worry.

'It must be.'

Her head shot up, and the worry disappeared in an instant, to be replaced by shock. 'I'd better stick to dogs. I wouldn't cope.'

What was going on? If he didn't know better he'd say Kate was overreacting to something she knew nothing about. There again, how well did he know her? 'I'd say most parents have to dig deep at times to cope with their children's problems and accidents. It must be normal.' He adjusted the X-ray machine over the dog's leg.

'Of course you're right. I was having a panic moment.'

'You have panic attacks?' he asked as he checked the screen to make sure he was taking a picture of exactly where the fracture appeared to be.

A blush crept into her perfect face, making her look vulnerable and even more beautiful. 'No.' She stepped back from the table so he could take the image. 'But I've always been a bit of a worrier when people or animals get hurt.'

Not quite a full answer, he suspected, but he'd let it go. It wasn't his place to start asking deep and meaningful questions. He'd like to know the answers, but then Kate would get the wrong idea and think he was trying to get close to her. Which couldn't be further from the truth. Either that, or he was lying to himself. 'Here. Come and look at this.' He stepped aside from the screen so he didn't have to breathe her scent.

Kate stared at the image. 'That needs surgery.'

'Yes. Can you put Rusty under while I get organised?'

'No problem.' She opened a cupboard and got out the required drug to administer.

Kate handed Finn a needle with suture thread to close the wound where he'd stitched the ligament back together in Rusty's leg. 'You're good.' Careful and exacting with his work. He'd just gone up a few notches in her view. Then there was the view of his alert eyes as he worked, and one thick blond curl that kept falling over his forehead that had her itching to shift it.

'This is my workmate's family.' Finn looked at her, his eyes crinkled at the corners. 'Can't send her boy home with any problems.'

For the first time since Charlotte had phoned, she laughed. Really laughed. She was probably being OTT with relief and drowning the stress that had gripped her, but she felt good. Her boy had a way to go. He'd suffer some pain and wouldn't be able to use that leg much for a while, but he'd eventually be running around again like the crazy dog he was. 'Now I know I can be a vet nurse if required. Though I know I'd want to interfere all the time.'

'We'd better get you both home. What if I drive Rusty home to your place and you take your car? Then I can carry him inside for you?'

She'd never finished her second drink at the pub so she'd be fine behind the wheel, and Rusty wasn't so heavy she couldn't lift him. 'Thanks, but I'll be fine. You've done more than enough already. I truly owe you a meal and beer now.'

'That won't be necessary.'

She shrugged at his sharp tone. 'We'll see.' He obviously wasn't pleased she'd turned down his offer of more help. But they'd spent more than enough time together tonight and the last thing she needed was Finn in her house, breathing the same air, taking up space with that long body, while she wandered around keeping an eye on her pet and reminding herself Finn was only there as a colleague. Not a prospective father of the children she wanted some day. That idea had slipped into her head when they were talking about dogs and families and she hadn't been able to get rid of it since. She'd always wanted a family and had thought Hamish was on the same page. Turned out he wasn't on the one about being faithful and loving his spouse for ever. 'I'll go and unlock the car.' Anything to get away from that look of annoyance coming her way. He'd be glad to see the back of her now.

But when she turned from the car to go back inside to get Rusty, Finn was walking towards her with her pet in his arms.

He was so caring and kind despite having been badly hurt. Her heart thumped once. She clenched her hands to prevent herself from leaning forward and kissing those sensual lips. Hell, she wanted to kiss him more than anything. To say thank you. To taste him again. To know him a little better.

Finn placed Rusty gently on the back seat and closed the door. 'I'll lock up. See you tomorrow.' Turning, he strode away.

Her heart crunched. Just like the first night when they'd met. Back straight and head high.

At least he hadn't said, 'I can't do this.' He had no idea how he affected her. Something to be grateful for. It would have been downright embarrassing if he'd known what she'd been thinking and feeling.

Kate's heart slammed shut.

I am not letting him in.

There was too much at stake. He might've been loving and careful with Rusty, but that wasn't enough to start letting go of her fear about being rejected yet again once he'd become intimate with her. Nothing would ever be enough to take that risk.

Inside the clinic, Finn scrubbed the operating table harder than necessary in an attempt to alleviate the frustration brought on by Kate damned Phillips. She'd sneaked under his skin without a blink. One moment they were chatting over a drink and the next he was tight for her. A tightness that hadn't abated ever since. Not even when she'd got the call about her dog. Seeing her pain and fear for her pet had only increased the longing filling him to be there for her.

Kate was in his head all the damned time. Laughing, being serious, caring for an animal, talking to patients and staff. She never left. Had he fallen a little bit in love with her when he was home seven months ago? Was that why he hadn't forgotten that kiss?

He tended to fall hard and fast. He had with Amelia anyway. A shiver tightened his skin. Kate was not Amelia. Except he didn't really know her that well. But she wouldn't be a vet if she were anything like Amelia. Vets were kind and caring people. And like him, she'd been on the receiving end of a lot of hurt from her ex. Was he messed up, or what? Only one thing was certain: he was not going to be sucked in and made a fool of ever again.

He hadn't forgotten the taste of Kate's lips under his when they'd kissed. Nor had he forgotten the sudden shock he'd experienced as he'd relaxed and felt excited while kissing her. It was the reason he'd abruptly walked away— to protect himself. He'd been blunt with her, and knew she'd been shocked about that, but there'd been no way he could follow up on that sensational kiss. He had shoved her out of his mind with a fierceness that suggested he'd tried too hard to forget her. It hadn't worked. There'd been weeks when he hadn't thought about her, but then there'd been many more times when she'd crept into his head to tease him, especially when he'd begun to think of returning home sooner than he'd originally been going to.

Now he was back permanently he needed to

deal with this before it became too difficult. He was not leaving home again. He'd missed it more than he cared to admit. Especially his family and friends. No one, not even Kate, was going to cause such havoc with his head or heart that he'd walk away from what was important to him again.

He threw the wipes in the bin, switched off lights, and headed outside. Time to get out of here and go home before any other distracting diversions cropped up.

When he pulled up outside the flat, the owner was crossing the lawn towards him as though he'd been waiting for him to get home. 'Hey, Finn, got a moment?'

It was well after ten. This couldn't be good. He opened the front door and flicked on some lights. 'What can I do for you, Harry?'

'Sorry to be the bearer of bad news, but the house has sold. The purchaser offered the price I was wanting if the property changes hands within two weeks.'

'You are kidding me.' Two weeks? It had taken a month to find this place. Unless he rented in the city—which he did not want to do—he was going to be hard pressed to find somewhere else in such a short time. There weren't a lot of rental properties around Darfield. So much for relaxing.

'I am really sorry, Finn, but you did know it was on the market.'

'I did.' He might get lucky and find somewhere quickly. Now that he'd started at the vet clinic, someone there might know of something available. 'I'm pleased for you, seeing as how your father needs to be in partial care.' He'd known the house had been on the market for more than six months, overpriced from what Finn had seen, but as he'd been desperate to settle somewhere he'd taken the flat. 'I must've brought you some luck.'

'Sorry, but them's the breaks. I'll ask around at work in case someone knows of a place available for rent.' Harry worked for a mechanical company in Darfield.

'Thanks, Harry.'

The man walked away, obviously relieved to have got his mission out of the way. He must've been dreading telling him, since he'd been waiting for Finn to come home.

Finn stepped inside and closed the door behind him before heading to the fridge and grabbing a beer. It was late but he wouldn't sleep anyway. First Kate playing with his mindset and now this. Maybe he should've stayed in Scotland, not come home to get on with turning his life around.

Sinking onto the couch and stretching his legs

out in front of him, he tipped his head back and stared up at the ceiling. 'It's a slight setback, nothing catastrophic.'

The cool beer took some of the heat out of his overactive mind. He'd sort it. It might even turn out to be for the best. Peter had mentioned some rural properties around Darfield and Kirwee had cottages that the owners rented out. One of those would be ideal, and way better than living in suburbia. Yes, he'd find somewhere else that he'd be happy to go home to at the end of the day. Absolutely.

'Wonder how Kate's feeling at the moment?' Hopefully Rusty was quiet and not causing her any more heartache.

It was too late to phone and find out. He had no idea what time she went to bed, but the hour was late. Bed. Kate. Instantly he was tight. The next mouthful of beer did nothing to cool him down. The image of that beautiful face and shapely body was doing a number on him. Leaping up, he grabbed his keys and headed outside, dropping the empty bottle in the recycle bin with a loud clang on the way past.

His steps ate up the footpath as he charged around West Melton, crossing streets, going along the grassed walkways, around the children's playground, out to the main road running between the city and Darfield, and still his body was tight. He did another circuit.

'Morning, Finn,' Kate greeted him late the next morning at the vet centre when he went in to write up notes on the cattle he'd been inspecting. 'You look tired.'

Lack of sleep did that. 'I'm good. How's Rusty?'

Her shoulders tightened. She must've got the message he wasn't in the mood for conversation and wasn't pleased with him. 'Sore and stiff but as hungry as usual. He's in one of the crates out the back. I don't want to leave him at home yet.'

'I can understand that.' She'd be worried if she wasn't around to watch over the dog. He sat down at the desk and clicked on the computer screen, focusing on work and not Kate, who thankfully left the room to call a dog and its owner into the treatment room. The sooner he got these notes done, the sooner he could leave and put some space between them.

But twenty minutes later she was standing in front of him. 'Finn, since you're here, do you think you could take a look at Rusty's leg for me? It's very red and looking a little swollen.'

'Of course. Give me a minute to finish this and I'll be there.' Why ask him when she was just as capable of dealing with the injury as he was?

'Thanks. I've looked at the wound and know

there's an infection brewing, but I'll feel a lot happier if you take a look in case there's anything I've missed. I'm probably overreacting but that's me.'

'Kate, you're a big softie.' Hadn't he said that last night? 'I do understand though.'

'Because you're a softie at heart too?' Her mouth lifted slightly.

He must be back in the good books. 'Who? Me? Not likely.' Only with those who were important to him. Plus the animals he treated. And Kate. No, not Kate. His hand gripped the mouse as he clicked hard on the X to close the screen. Yes, Kate.

Shoving back the chair, he stood up.

Kate was heading down the hall to the room where animals were put in crates while coming round after surgery or some other treatment.

He followed slowly. There hadn't been a lot of sleep last night. Funny thing was that it was Kate who had kept him awake, not the fact he had to find somewhere else to live in a hurry.

She was lifting Rusty onto the table when he entered the room.

'Hey, I could've done that.' He liked to do his bit, and helping a colleague was right up there. Except that, while he did work with Kate, she was more than a colleague. She was a friend in the making. That was it. A friend. Nothing more.

'I'm good.'

Didn't he know it? 'When did you look at Rusty's leg?' The crepe bandage was loose.

'Half an hour ago. He'd been whimpering more than he had earlier, and I like to keep an eye on injuries for any animal I'm working with.'

'Especially your own pet.'

'Yeah.' Her gaze was fixed on his hands as he unwound the bandage and exposed the red wound site.

Glancing up, he saw that her teeth were digging into her bottom lip. He mock growled. 'Don't do that, Kate. Rusty's going to be fine once I give him some more antibiotics. So far the infection's mild. I'll give him a heavy dose to stop it in its tracks.' He looked firmly at Kate. 'If that's all right with you.'

'It's what I'd do.' She rubbed the dog's head so softly Finn wanted to touch her in a similar way to reassure her all would go well with the surgical site.

Of course, he resisted. 'I'll fetch the injection and get this done. Have you got any more appointments this morning?'

'One more at midday. A schnauzer with grass-seed allergies needs a top-up of corticosteroid.' Kate suddenly looked all-in.

Could be he wasn't the only one who'd missed out on sleep last night. 'Want me to stay and do that? I've got nothing on for the rest of the day.' Other than talking to letting agencies about rental properties, and he could do that while sitting in Reception waiting for the schnauzer.

Back to that lip-nibbling thing, Kate looked from Rusty to him. Something was bugging her.

'What's up? You look as though you've got a problem.'

Her ponytail slid from side to side when she shook her head. 'Not really. If you're serious about dealing with the last appointment, then I'll take you up on your offer. Thanks.'

'Sorted. You get out of here while you can.' He saw her rub her lower back and stepped closer to the table and Rusty. 'Go and open your car. I'll bring this fella out.' The dog could walk but it would be awkward and painful for Rusty and Kate, and *he* wanted to do something more than seeing to her final appointment for her.

When Kate didn't argue he had to wonder what was bothering her, but he refrained from asking as the answer might be something he didn't want to hear. They were getting on fine and he didn't want to mess with that. As he followed her out to the car, longing for a deeper relationship sprang up. Kate was lovely, inside and out. The kind of woman he could lose his head over. Right now he should be putting the dog down and running for the hills. Except he really didn't want to. Despite all the warnings he'd gone through while striding around West Melton last night, he did not want to turn his back on Kate.

So he placed the spaniel on the back seat, closed the door, and headed back inside without another word.

CHAPTER FIVE

'THERE YOU GO, RUSTY. All snug and dry.' Kate closed the crate and stood up. She could've left her pet at home in the laundry room with Sam but she liked to be able to keep an eye on him. The wound was healing well and he did use the injured leg at the moments when there were interesting objects to pursue in the yard, but she'd spend the day worrying he'd hurt himself if she left him at home.

'How's the infection?' Finn asked from the doorway.

'Clearing up fast.'

'Glad to hear it.' Finn sounded more relaxed this morning than he had on Saturday. He must've had a good weekend. 'Peter's in the tearoom waiting for everyone to turn up.'

'Coming.' They opened up half an hour later for patients on Mondays so everyone could get together to discuss any problems that had arisen over the past week.

'I've made your coffee,' Finn told her.

'Thanks.' Following him into the staff room, she felt good. The weekend had been quiet. She'd visited her parents and helped her dad bottle too many kilos of tomatoes. Now, seeing Finn looking so at ease and as handsome as ever was warming her throughout. Not that he was supposed to do that. Friendly colleagues only. Easier said, apparently.

Finn went to the bench and picked up two full mugs. 'Here you go.'

Taking her drink, she sat down next to Peter, and, when Finn took the seat on the opposite side of him, sighed with relief. She was getting used to having him around, just as she'd intended from the start, but it was difficult to remain calm at the times when he sat next to her. If only she could ignore the humming in her veins. He got to her all too quickly. 'Morning, Peter. How was your weekend?'

'If you don't count the fact that the motor mower blew a couple of valves, then perfect.' Peter grinned. 'A mechanic I am not.'

'You should've called round and got mine,' Kate told him.

'And spoil a quiet afternoon? No, thanks. Seriously, the mower will be back in working order later today.' He looked around. 'Still waiting for Mark, I see.'

'He's dealing to a cat that's had a claw torn out,' Di said. 'He said to go ahead without him.'

'Right, then let's get on with things.' Peter filled them in on progress with the school pet fair arrangements. 'That's about it from me. Anyone got something to tell us?'

A lot of head shaking went on around the table.

'Good. The only other thing I want to mention is that Finn is looking for a place to rent, so if anyone knows of somewhere, or hears of one, please let him know.' Peter turned to Kate. 'You haven't taken in anyone since your last boarder left, have you?'

'No-o.' Finn was the last person she wanted living under her roof. They were getting along well but she couldn't see that going quite as smoothly if they spent more time together. She'd have to be ultra cautious and when it was in her own home and the one place she could relax completely, it wasn't a good idea.

'That could be an answer to your predicament, Finn.'

Shut up, Peter.

She glanced at Finn and saw his jaw tighten. This was the man who'd leapt in to help her with Rusty on Friday. The guy who'd taken her to the pub for a drink and a meal. He'd been nothing but good to her, though often a little edgy. 'You can take a look at the room if you'd like,' she said in a rush. 'It's got a bed and dresser so you wouldn't need to bring any furniture.'

His chest rose and fell. 'Thanks, Kate. It's good of you to offer but I've got every agent in the area on my case so hopefully something should turn up soon.'

Fingers crossed he was right. She'd heard that he'd had difficulty finding a place last time and it hadn't been more than a few weeks ago so chances were he would have the same problem now. 'Why are you moving out of the flat you already had?'

'It's been sold and the purchaser offered a good deal if the property changed hands quickly. To be honest, I did agree to a short time frame to get out if it sold and in return had a lower rent so I can't complain.' His smile was rueful. 'Silly me.'

Finn was not silly. Far from it. 'Here's hoping you find a place you like.' Deep breath. He'd know she wasn't keen on him moving in. She doubted he'd be that willing either. 'If not, you are welcome to use my spare room.'

Looking around to make sure everyone had left the room, Finn leaned back in his chair. 'Thank you, Kate, but we both know we're still trying to make this work so that we're comfortable around here, and sharing a house would only add to the pressure.'

Or it could go some way towards cementing their friendship, except she wasn't so sure about that. 'I thought we were getting along fine.' If she didn't think about how she'd wanted to kiss him the other night. She could be grateful he'd left before her feelings had really taken over and she'd made a fool of herself. She was not prepared to face that a second time from Finn. Or anyone.

Di appeared in the room. 'Finn, your first visit's been cancelled. I've rung Monty to see if you could go to his farm earlier than arranged but he's in town at the moment so you've got nothing on for the next hour or so.'

'Guess that means I'll hang around here and give Kate and Mark a hand. They seem to have a long list of patients this morning.'

Kate was on her feet. 'We do. I don't know what it is about Mondays, but it's nothing unusual. Can you take one of Mark's as he's obviously busy with that cat?'

'On to it.'

So Finn needed accommodation sooner rather than later. He had to find somewhere else. It was a bad idea for him to move in, but there wasn't a lot she could do about it now that she'd made the offer. It was up to Finn what he did with it.

She followed him out of the room and went to get her first patient. 'Barb, come through with Jetson.'

A middle-aged woman led her Alsatian into the treatment room and got him up to sit on the examination table. 'How's things, Kate? Busy as usual?'

'You bet. No rest for vets.' She laughed, a little tightly but she was wearing her professional face.

'I hear there's a new vet started here. Quite a looker apparently.'

Word got around fast in small towns. 'Finn Anderson. He's mostly doing farm animals but, having said that, he's working in here this morning.' That'd give Barb someone to look out for and satisfy her interest. 'Now, what's up with Jetson?'

'He's not eating properly. It started last week and first I thought he'd eaten something bad, but after two days I decided it had to be something else. He doesn't have much energy.'

Jetson wasn't on any medications, nor had he had a vaccination recently, so she could rule those out as causes. 'I'll check his body for pain in case he's injured internally.' As she felt over the dog's stomach and ribs she asked Barb, 'Has he been stressed about anything out of the ordinary lately?'

'Not that I've noticed.' And Barb would. Her dog was the most important part of her life.

Jetson was remaining still, his eyes watching Kate's every move. 'Any changes to what you feed him?'

'No.' Worry was building up in Barb's face.

'No fractures or internal wounds as far as I can ascertain.' She'd do an X-ray if no reason for the lack of appetite showed up. 'I'll check his teeth now. Not chewing can be a sign of a broken tooth or an infection in the gums.'

'He hasn't touched a bone for more than a week.'

That should've been the first thing Barb mentioned but Kate understood what it was like to be stressed about your four-footed buddies, and this woman didn't have Finn around to make sure her pet was given the best going-over. Finn. His name slipped silently across her lips. He'd been brilliant with Rusty. He'd also fully understood how she'd been hurting for her boy. She wriggled each of Jetson's teeth, moving slowly along the bottom row then the top.

Suddenly Jetson jerked his head away. 'Grr.'

Pulling away, Kate said, 'Think we know what's causing the loss of appetite. The last tooth I touched was loose, but there could be more. I'm going to sedate him before I go any further.' Putting her fingers inside a distressed dog's mouth while he was fully awake was not an option now she knew where the problem lay. 'I'll get Di to give me a hand.'

Returning with the nurse, Kate told her what was required. 'Is the operating room free this morning?'

'Yes,' Di said. 'Until eleven when you've got two cats to de-sex and a metal pin to remove from the leg of a sheepdog.'

'Then I can use the room now if necessary. I'll take this guy in there shortly. Finn can take over some of my appointments once Mark's ready to do his.' Sometimes things worked out well, when she wasn't thinking how she preferred Finn wasn't in the building. If he'd been out in the field as he was meant to be Jetson would have had to wait until she'd finished her operating schedule to have his problem dealt with. It wouldn't have been an issue but she liked to keep animals calm and comfortable, and giving him too much sedative while waiting wasn't good when she had to put him under later.

Within moments of the sedative being dispensed into the back of his neck, Jetson was asleep, and Kate could examine his mouth thoroughly. 'Two loose teeth and swelling in the gum along with an infection. I'll take an X-ray to find the cause.'

As she rubbed her pet's back, Barb asked, 'Will you be removing teeth?'

'It's very likely, but until I can see exactly what the problem is I don't know what I'll be doing. It could be that he's got a slither of bone stuck in his gum that's causing an infection.'

'Sounds like surgery might be necessary.'

'Yes, it could be.' With Di's help Kate took Jetson through to the room next door to x-ray his mouth.

When she returned without the dog, Barb's face crumpled. 'You're going to operate.'

'There is something embedded in his gum between the two loose teeth that has to be removed if we're to stop the pain and the infection. Are you okay with me carrying on?'

'Just do it. Make him happy again.'

'Di will bring you a form to fill in and sign. We'll keep Jetson here for the day, and I'll phone you as soon as I've finished the surgery to let you know how it went.'

Finn walked in. 'I hear you want me to carry on with your patients now that Mark's back on board with his.'

'That would be helpful.' Of course, as the clinic manager she could've just said that was what he'd be doing, but it wasn't her style. 'Finn, this is Barb Newton. It's her Alsatian's mouth I'm going to remove an obstruction from.'

'H-hello, Finn. I heard you'd started here. Welcome to Darfield.' Barb's face was turning pink.

Kate knew all too well what that was like.

'Thank you, Barb. It's a great area to be in, and the practice is excellent. You've brought Jetson to the right place.' He smiled and Barb's colour deepened.

'I—I'd better sign the form you mentioned, Kate, and get out of your way.' Barb turned for the door.

Finn reached over to open it for her.

Kate was laughing to herself. The man was hot, and, it seemed, setting off firecrackers in lots of women. 'I like your advertising. Never hurts to put us out there.'

'If I get bored being a vet, I'll know what to do next for a career.' He grinned.

'You'll never get fed up with veterinary work. You're passionate about it.'

His grin widened as he tilted his head to one side. 'You think?'

'I know.' Kate turned away before her face outdid Barb's for colour. Damn him for being able to tip her off centre so easily—with a grin. What happened to never letting a man get close again? They *weren't* close. No, but keep up these thoughts and the feelings that came with them and there'd be no stopping her trying to get there. Heck, he could not move into her house. No way. She'd never keep her distance. Unless he saw her scars and then he'd be gone. Out of her life for ever. She'd have to pull on her big girl's hat once more and pretend it didn't hurt, when it always hurt—badly.

'Kate? You all right?'

'I'm fine, thinking about what I have to do with Jetson.'

'Try again, Kate. You're not fooling me one little bit.'

Fighting the urge to throw herself at Finn just because he understood her a little too well, she turned slowly. 'We need to get back to work, Finn.'

'You're right. We do.' The disappointment coming her way was huge.

In looking out for herself, she'd let him down. He was vulnerable too. She'd never deliberately hurt him, but with her insecurities it wouldn't be hard to do. More than ever before, she couldn't stand the thought of Finn's eyes widening in horror and awful words spilling from that beautiful mouth. 'I'm sorry.' She'd hurt them both. Like it or not, she was starting to care too much for Finn and every step came with a price. Most of which she was afraid to incur, for fear of having her heart broken a second time.

Finn watched Kate walk into the room next door and swallowed hard. By walking away she'd done the right thing by him. She was saving his heart, whether she knew it or not. He was more than a little smitten with her, but that did not ease the fear of being used and decimated again. Returning home because he missed his family and friends was all very well, as was starting to get on with making a life for himself in the one place he wanted to live permanently. But that wasn't easy. Far from it.

Without even trying, he was unwittingly edging beyond the boundaries he had set. All because Kate often managed to make him forget his fears momentarily. It was not wise. Sooner or later his trust would be tested and he had none to give. If Amelia could knowingly rob him of love, and of everything he possessed, and of his self-worth, then he'd be an absolute fool to risk it again. Even worse was how she'd offered him hope in following up on the dream to have a family and then taken it away with her horrific confession. 'I am not pregnant, never was. That positive test was not mine. You were an idiot to believe it was real.' Talk about a deal-breaker. How could he ever trust a woman with his heart again?

That he'd never forgotten what it had felt like to hold Kate and kiss her the night he'd met her even once he'd been back on the other side of the world was huge. But it didn't change anything. He was not ready to follow through. He'd never be.

'Finn, you've got two people with their pets waiting to see you.' Kate had returned.

Did she know what he was thinking? Was he easy to read? Of course not. He was being paranoid. 'I'll be right there.'

'I'll take one before I see to Jetson.'

He shook his head. 'That won't be necessary.' When her eyes began to widen, he nodded. 'Seriously, I'm not going to let the team down. I was just having a moment of indecision, but I'm sorted.' For now, at least.

Her face softened. 'Nothing's ever easy, is it? I'm sure you'll get your accommodation sorted in no time.'

Her misunderstanding was a relief. 'I will.'

Hopefully not by moving in with you, Kate, because I'm starting to see I'd never handle having you so near all the time.

It was bad enough bumping into her at work, but then he got to go home, and she wasn't anywhere in sight. Except when he went and invited her to the pub, and ended up at her house and then bringing her dog here to operate on.

Checking the screen to see which person to call in, he headed out to the waiting room while Di wiped down the table from the last animal. 'Pauline Clark?'

A young woman stood up and lifted a cat crate from the chair beside her. 'That's me, and this is Scratch.'

'I'm Finn Anderson, your vet for this visit. Come through.'

Pauline was eying him up. 'I heard about you when I dropped the kids off at school. Everyone seems to know there's a new vet in town.'

She could look all she liked, but being single didn't mean he was interested. The point was, he'd made himself unavailable to protect himself, and keeping Kate at bay was hard enough. No other woman would be able to unsettle him the way she did, so it was easy to walk into the treatment room with Pauline and not really notice her other than as a cat's owner. 'So what's Scratch's problem?'

'He's losing fur non-stop,' Pauline said as she lifted the tabby from the crate and held him in her arms.

Finn took the cat and placed him on the table so he could get a better look.

Di moved up and held Scratch still, which was good because Finn didn't feel like having claws ripping his skin through his gloves. 'There are quite a few bald patches. Have you changed his diet recently?'

'Yes. He seemed to be less energetic so I got

a different brand of biscuits about four weeks ago,' Pauline answered.

'Did that improve his energy levels?'

'A little. Then the fur started coming away in clumps, but I didn't think about the biscuits being a reason for that.'

'There's no sign of ringworm, which could've been a cause.' No allergies were recorded in the cat's file, and Scratch wasn't on any medications. 'I suggest you take him off those particular biscuits and go back to the original ones. Also I can recommend some other foods to boost his energy levels.' Finn glanced at the screen in front of him. 'He's getting on in years so it could be he's slowing down.'

'Shh. He'll hear you.' Pauline laughed, then said more seriously, 'Thank you so much. You've made me feel a lot happier. I'll give away the biscuits and buy whatever it is you're suggesting.'

'Di, show Pauline the options we've got so she can get Scratch started.'

'Will do.' Di lifted Scratch off the table and cuddled him. 'Come on, little man. Let's get you something yummy to eat.' Which meant Di would give the cat one of the treats she kept at her desk.

As Finn made his way back out to Reception for the next patient, he heard Kate talking and laughing in the operating room. Was someone else in there with her? He couldn't hear anyone. Maybe she was talking to her unconscious patient. That way she wouldn't get answers she didn't want to hear. He smiled to himself at the zing in his step. He shouldn't feel like this, but there was no stopping him. Kate did that to him. He hated to admit it, but it seemed he didn't have a lot of control over his emotions when it came to her. So moving in with her was out. A cave would be safer.

Right, get on with what he was here for. 'Jonathon Bell?' Not Kate Phillips.

An elderly man stood up with a leash in hand that was attached to a mixed breed, mid-sized dog. 'That's us.'

'Come through.' Finn closed the door to the waiting room behind them, and shut his mind down on all things Kate and his future, and got on with work. It was the only way to get through the day and come out sane.

That or a phone call from a rental agent telling him they'd found him somewhere to live.

CHAPTER SIX

'ANOTHER WEEK FINISHED.' Kate raised her glass to everyone sitting around the table in the tea-room after the front door had been locked behind the last animal needing attention for the day. 'It's been a busy one.' She was more tired than usual. A glance in Finn's direction reminded her how often she'd lain in bed throughout the week thinking about him. At least he hadn't been across the hall in the other bedroom or who knew what she might've done?

'It certainly has,' Mark agreed before taking a mouthful of his beer. 'Glad it's you on call, Kate.'

'What's everyone got planned for the weekend?' Finn asked.

'Anything that has nothing to do with sick animals,' Peter retorted, then grinned. 'As little as possible.'

'You know what we haven't done for a while?' Kate asked before putting her brain in gear. 'When was the last time we had a staff barbecue?'

'About two months ago,' Di answered. 'Want to have another?'

So much for thinking straight. She'd really blown her determination to keep Finn at arm's length. But she could hardly say no now. 'Let's. We can have it at my place.' Because that was what they usually did. 'If I get called out it's not as though you don't all know your way around.'

Strangely the idea was perking her up, shoving the exhaustion aside. It was something to look forward to. She could see more of Finn without being alone with him. That had to be good for a lot of reasons. Or possibly not. He'd get to see her home and how she lived. But if he moved in, he'd learn even more about her. Anyway, she couldn't retract the offer of her spare room any more than she could the suggestion of a staff get-together.

'I'm on,' Di said.

'Count me and Sheree in,' Peter added.

'We'll be there,' Mark said.

Kate went round the table, getting the same answer from everyone, including Finn, who asked, 'How does this work? Do we all bring meat and salads?'

As Kate went to explain her phone rang. It was the clinic number, which had been switched over to her phone. 'Here we go.' Stepping away, she said, 'Hello, this is Kate Phillips at Darfield Animal Care.'

'Kate, Dave Crocker. There's been an accident on the West Coast Road involving a horse float with two horses on board. Can you come?'

The local cop sounded stressed. 'On my way, Dave. Can you tell me how far along the road the accident happened?'

Heads turned and everyone was suddenly quiet, listening to her side of the conversation.

'About twenty k's from town,' Dave told her. 'I don't think the horses are in good nick.'

Wonderful. As she listened she mentally ran through her kit, making certain everything she could possibly need was there, including sodium pentobarbital in case she had to put either of the horses down. Not that her kit wouldn't have everything but she could never be too sure. 'See you shortly.' Hanging up, she turned to the others. 'That was Dave. A small truck spun into a four-wheel drive towing a horse float. Two horses have been injured, possibly critically. I'm off.'

Finn was on his feet in a shot. 'I'm coming with you.'

As she opened her mouth to say he didn't need to, he cut her off.

'Two badly injured horses? Two vets are better than one.'

She couldn't argue with that. 'Grab your gear. We're out of here.' As she headed away, she called over her shoulder, 'Someone fill me in later about the barbecue. You know I'm happy with anything going.'

'I'll text you,' Di returned.

Her car was already running when Finn leapt into the front seat. 'Any more details than what you said inside?'

'Dave thinks one horse might have a broken leg, but he added it's mayhem in the float and no one's game enough to get close enough to find out what injuries the animals have.'

'What about the driver towing the float?'

'An ambulance is on its way for her. She was thrown through the windscreen. It must've been a massive impact.' When Kate hit the main road she pressed hard on the accelerator. Dave had said 'don't dally' so he'd back her if one of his colleagues tried to stop her.

'Sounds like the truck hit her vehicle very hard,' Finn commented, unaware she'd had a similar thought. Then he tightened his seat belt.

'It's all right. I won't go too fast, but Dave sounded extremely worried and the fact the horses are kicking and trying to get out of the float means we need to get there as soon as safely possible.'

'I'm all good, Kate. I want to get there asap too.'

They didn't talk much after that. Kate was concentrating on driving and Finn went through his kit to find vials of xylazine to help with the pain the horses would be in. 'How we're going to administer this when they're so restless is something to think about.'

'I don't fancy being kicked,' Kate agreed. 'Out of my way,' she growled at a slow campervan, and, glad they were on a straight stretch of road, indicated before pulling out to pass. The kilometres were disappearing but it seemed to take for ever to reach the accident site. Finally she spied red and blue lights flashing on top of a cop car. Easing off the pedal, she heaved a sigh of relief. 'Now the real fun starts.'

Finn placed his hand over hers. 'We've got this.'

In other words, they were together, a team. A good team. That made her feel happy. So did the feel of his warmth on her hand. 'We have.' Pulling over onto the grass, she pulled on the brake and shut off the engine. 'That's Dave coming our way. Have you met him yet?'

'No, I haven't.'

'He's a good guy. Believes in being there when people are in dire straits, and also has a firm hand when it comes to dealing with out-of-control teenagers.'

'I like him already,' Finn said as he pushed out of the car.

'Kate, the horses have quietened a little but everyone's staying back in case they get upset again. The owner, Doria, is in the ambulance, and her husband's on his way here to see what's going on with the horses.' Dave nodded over at Finn. 'Hello, I take it you're the new vet?'

Finn stepped around the car with his hand extended. 'Finn Anderson. Pleased to meet you, though not in the circumstances I'd prefer.'

Kate wasn't hanging around to play nice and friendly. The plight of the horses was worrying her. The fact they'd quietened more likely meant shock was taking hold, and they could still react violently when approached. Unfortunately there was no avoiding that she and Finn did have to get close to administer drugs and see what the injuries were.

As she reached the float Finn touched her elbow to indicate he was right there with her. His second light touch since they'd arrived. She'd never felt the need to have another vet alongside her when faced with a serious accident involving animals, but his touches calmed the turmoil in her belly so she could focus better on what was important.

The float was on its side. Plywood and fibre-glass were strewn everywhere, as were the aluminium sheets that had once kept the horses protected inside. A lump formed in her chest as she regarded the two mares sprawled in the carnage, their legs twitching and their mouths frothing. One was on her side, while the other was seated on her butt and trying to stand, groaning in agony.

'This doesn't look good.' She took a couple of steps closer, Finn with her. Pointing to the closest horse, she said, 'I'll take this one.' Placing her kit on the ground, she leaned over the mare trying to stand, and made observations of the breathing rate, heartbeat, and then began assessing the mare's body externally without touching her, and all the time aware of her movements. Fortunately those were getting weaker as the pain and shock took over. Not that Kate wanted the animal to be suffering those. 'Back right leg fractured. Ribcage compressed.' There were bleeding abrasions in many places but those weren't urgent.

'Fractured left back leg, and possibly the left front leg on this one,' Finn replied moments later. 'There's also an indentation on her head on the same side.'

Kate locked eyes with him. None of this boded well. 'Pain relief first.'

His nod was brief. 'Let's do one at a time so we can assist each other in case either horse reacts badly.' He didn't add that they'd be in a direct line for trouble if that happened.

'This one first. She's still jumpy.'

Finn delved in the kit and held up the syringe and xylazine. 'Agreed?'

'Yes.' Carefully reaching over to the horse's neck, Kate found the triangular spot used for injections and reached behind her for the needle Finn was holding out. Under her hand, the horse flinched and raised her head a few inches. 'Shh, it's okay, girl. We're going to help with the pain.' She held her breath as she slid the needle under the skin, her heart beating heavily as she squeezed the plunger and hoped like crazy the mare didn't jerk her head around or try to get away from her. Within seconds she was withdrawing the needle and sitting back on her haunches, sweat beading between her eyebrows. 'Phew.'

Finn said, 'Well done.'

'One done, next one coming up.'

'My turn to be in the firing line.' Finn stood up, reaching down to help her up too. He gave her hand a small squeeze before getting the second syringe and ampule and moving close to the mare. As he leaned down the horse's nostrils flared and she banged a hoof on the ground. 'It's all right. I'm here to help you.' His voice was so soft Kate smiled. If only he were holding her.

Tyres screeched on the road and then a door was slammed shut.

The mare hesitated, her head still as she appeared to be listening, and Finn made the most of the opportunity. He had the needle in her neck fast and pressed down to empty the drug into the horse, then stood up to step back.

A man appeared beside Kate. 'What's happening? Are the horses in a bad way?'

'Are you the owner's husband?' Kate asked.

'Yes, I am. I should be on the way to the hospital but someone had to come and deal with this mess.'

It must be hard for the man. Kate immediately got down to business. 'I'm Kate Phillips, a vet from Darfield, and this is Finn Anderson, a vet from the same practice. We have just given both horses painkillers. One has two broken legs and other injuries, and the second one has a fractured leg and possibly broken ribs.'

The man swore. When he calmed, he said, 'Sorry but this is a nightmare. Doria dotes on these two. How am I going to tell her what's happened?' It seemed he might understand what probably lay ahead.

These horses weren't going to get back up on their feet without major surgery and a very long recovery, and even then it wouldn't be an easy process for the animals. Kate glanced at Finn, who grimaced, before saying to the man, 'There is a possibility of operating and placing pins in their legs but in reality that's going to be very hard on the mares. If there are multiple fractures around the site, then I wouldn't recommend it.'

Kate added, 'We won't know what we're faced with until X-rays are done.' Which wouldn't be easy. 'For that the horses need to be moved onto trailers and taken away from here to their stables.' They'd need to be unconscious during the process of moving them.

The man stared at the mares. 'I'm Colin. Sorry, didn't say earlier.' He knelt down beside one mare. 'Hey, Cass, girl, I'm here.' He reached out to stroke her.

'Careful,' Kate warned. 'They're not their usual selves.'

But Cass didn't flinch. She obviously knew Colin's touch. He looked up at Kate. 'You're going to have to euthanise them.'

Was that a demand or a question? 'The odds point that way, but it's not my call. You and your wife need to decide how far you want to take these mares in terms of treatment and how they'll get around during the coming months.' Her heart was hurting for the couple and their mares. She hated the days when she had to put an animal down. It never got any easier.

The man stood up. 'Decision made. I can't

bear the thought of these two in pain and probably never getting back the full use of their legs.
See to it, will you? I'm going to the hospital to
be with Doria.'

'Hang on, mate.' Dave stepped up. 'There's
the matter of getting the horses moved away
from here.'

'It'll have to wait. I need to see Doria and
make sure she's all right.'

'Is there someone you can call to come sort
this out?'

'What about these vets?'

As Kate opened her mouth to explain they
didn't do that, Dave said, 'It's not their job.
They'll euthanise the horses but someone else
has to remove the animals and the remains of
the float from the roadside.'

'I'll call our neighbour to come with his trailer
and a couple of guys to help him,' Colin croaked.

Finn had his kit open. 'I'll give each mare another sedative. Then I'll follow up with the sodium pentobarbital.'

A second sedative wasn't going to harm the
horses, and would prevent any movement if either of them got stressed again. 'I'll take care of
this one,' Kate told him. She might hate doing
this but she wasn't about to leave it all to Finn.
That was hardly fair. The sadness in his eyes told
her he felt much the same as she did. Then again,

find a vet who didn't and that person shouldn't be in the job.

Colin coughed. 'Thanks, both of you. It's hard, you know? I've got to tell Doria.' He was choked up, and his eyes were watery.

'Go and make that call, Colin,' Kate said. He didn't need to watch the process. 'Then get on the road to the hospital.' She moved away and took the syringe with an attached sedative capsule from Finn. 'Thanks.' On her knees, she kept a firm eye on Cass as she rubbed the spot on her neck where she'd insert the last needle. 'Good girl. Just a small prick and you'll go to sleep.'

Then another prick and you'll never wake up again.

Kate blinked. Focused. It was necessary but awful all the same.

Back at the clinic, Finn took both kits inside to top up the drugs and syringes they'd used. Night had fallen and everyone had left for home. He felt flat after euthanising those mares. This was when he liked having others around to lift his spirits. 'Kate, once we've done this, feel like a wine since we didn't get to finish the first one?' He'd do whatever it took to keep her here a bit longer, and hopefully put a smile on her wan face while lifting his own spirits.

'Best idea ever.' The front door closed with a bang. 'I'm not ready to go home yet.'

'We could go to the pub for a meal.' That'd keep her at his side for a while longer. Then he sighed. Talk about sounding desperate. But it had been a long time since he'd had that special person he could download with. Tonight it would be different because Kate had been there with him, and had had to do the same thing to one of the mares.

'I'm not hungry.' She took the vials he handed her and placed them in her kit. Her voice sounded as flat as he felt.

'Time for a career in banking?' he quipped in an attempt to lift the mood between them.

'Think I'll try my hand at commercial gardening. Only thing that'd die would be the plants.'

'Aww, Kate. Come here.' Finn took her in his arms and held her tight. 'This side of the job's a bitch.'

'Totally.'

Her body folded into his and her arms went around his waist. Her head lay on his chest and he could feel her breaths at the vee of his shirt. Damn, he'd missed this. Worse, he hadn't even realised it hadn't been there. He'd been so focused on putting Amelia and the past behind him that he hadn't thought about anything else. Now he was looking ahead and it wasn't quite

as bad as he'd thought. There might even be opportunities for happiness—and love. He stood
straighter, pulled back.

'Finn?' The beautiful face that filled his mind
at all sorts of moments was looking up at him
with puzzlement. 'What's going on in your
mind?'

*Wouldn't you like to know? You'd probably
run for your car and speed away if I told you.*

'It was hard dealing with the horses so I was
relaxing with you.'

'Then you stopped.'

'I'm not sure if holding you is the right thing
to be doing.' He could do honest with this
woman far too easily. About some things anyway. It was those other things that frightened
him. Mentioning how good she made him feel
would be a game-changer he wasn't prepared
for. 'Let's have that wine.'

Pushing up onto her toes, she brushed a light
kiss on his mouth. 'I'll get it.' She walked away
from him.

Was that disappointment on her face because
he'd been honest? Surely not. That'd suggest she
had similar feelings to his about having someone to share tragic events with and that didn't
make sense. But she'd kissed him—softly, and
so tantalisingly he wanted more. More kisses
and more of her company.

Was Kate taking a shine to him? Did she want something stronger than a workplace friendship? He should've said he'd changed his mind about having a wine but for the life of him he couldn't find it in him to do so. Spending time with Kate was starting to feel too good. She brought him alive in ways he hadn't known for a long while, ways he'd been intent on denying himself to remain safe.

He wasn't only thinking about sex but also about sharing the things that made a real life. A home, family and friends. Those were what he'd grown up believing in, only to have the possibility slashed from under him. Yet here he was opening up ever so slightly to thinking he might find them all because Kate had a way of sneaking under his radar.

Her voice interrupted the errant thoughts. 'Unfortunately we didn't really have any choice. The two mares were in a serious condition. The owner's husband gave us the go-ahead.' Kate pointed to her phone and mouthed 'Peter' to him.

He took the bottle out of her hand and found two glasses in the cupboard to fill.

'No, it wasn't pleasant.' Kate paused, listening to Peter. 'Great. I'm looking forward to it. Sounds like there'll be way too much food as usual.' She wasn't smiling. Her mind was most likely still on the mares and not tomorrow night's barbecue. Or could she be thinking about kissing him again? Yes, please.

When Kate placed her phone on the table Finn handed her a glass. 'Get some of that inside you.'

'Oh, Finn, it never gets any easier, does it?' She wiped a tear from her cheek.

'Nope, afraid not.' Leaning closer, he wiped a second tear from her other cheek. 'But you were kind and gentle with Cass. That's what counts.'

Kate watched him as she took a large mouthful of wine, her eyes filled with a longing he didn't dare put a name to.

He took a sip of his drink and placed the glass on the table beside him, not looking away from Kate's gaze for a second.

Kate leaned sideways and put her glass down too, still watching him.

Simultaneously they reached for each other, their mouths meeting, touching, tasting, feeding that longing he'd seen in her eyes and known inside his heart. This was Kate, the woman who'd played with his mind for months, the woman he'd kissed once before and never forgotten what it had felt like.

Kate.

He tightened his hold around her, drew her even closer so her breasts were pressed against his chest, her stomach pushing into him. She was wonderful.

Kate's tongue was on his, sending his need spiralling out of control. Her lips were soft under his. Her hands firm on his butt. He was in paradise, returning the kiss with everything he had.

It wasn't enough. He needed to feel her skin, to touch those breasts, to get even closer. 'Kate?' he whispered against her mouth.

Her lips sealed against his again, kissing him back fervently. Then Kate lifted a leg up to his waist, then the other, and her arms were around his shoulders. 'Take me, Finn.'

His eyes popped open and he looked at her. 'You have no idea how much I want you.'

'What's stopping you?'

'Nothing.' Holding that wonderful body tight against him, he carried her into the office and closed the door to keep the world out. He didn't bother with lights. He could find his way around Kate so easily it was wonderful. It wasn't the wisest thing he'd done but there was no stopping the need pouring through him. And, he suspected as Kate kissed his neck and chin, no stopping her either.

As she slid down his body to stand before him, her hands were reaching for his trousers, undoing the zip to take hold of his erection. One touch and he was nearly gone. 'Stop, Kate. We're doing this together.'

She grabbed his hand and placed it against her moist centre.

When had she discarded her trousers? Touching her heat sent sparks flying throughout his taut body, teasing, tantalising. Damn she was amazing. So sexy. He was losing control far too quickly.

'Finn, lift me up against the wall so I can ride you.'

Then she was holding onto him and sliding down over him and he was brushing her heat and they were coming together.

The next thing he knew was Kate cuddled up against him with the wall at her back and her short breaths hot against his chest. 'Kate.' He stopped. What could he say that would be better than what had just gone down between them? Nothing. He brushed a kiss over her forehead, then another on her lips.

She stared at him and a sensual smile grew on those lips. 'Wow.'

'Yes, wow.' He stepped back and pulled his trousers up from around his ankles.

Suddenly Kate jerked, and reached for her trousers too, turning her back slightly as she did.

'Kate? You all right?'

'Couldn't be better.' She tossed him a crooked smile over her shoulder, then zipped her trousers and turned back to face him looking a little confused.

'You're not regretting this already?' He'd be gutted if she was. Though he knew he had done something he'd sworn not to, he did not regret it at all. How could he when Kate was so wonderful?

'No, Finn, I am not. It's only that we're supposed to be friendly colleagues and nothing more.'

He laughed. 'Friendly colleagues? Is that how you see us?'

'I did. And if we're to continue working side by side it might be the only way to go.' Her smile dimmed. 'Except I can't imagine that any more. Not after what I've just experienced with you.'

'One day—or should that be kiss—at a time, eh?'

Her shoulders lifted, fell away again. But her smile remained. 'Deal.'

'Come here.' He wrapped his arms around her and held her close and tight. He hadn't felt so comfortable with a woman in a long time. Not even the few he'd dated on and off in Scotland had given him a sense of belonging. Which was downright scary. But he couldn't pull away. Not yet. He had to hold Kate just a little bit longer first.

Then the phone spoilt everything by ringing loud and clear.

'At least whoever it is didn't call ten minutes ago,' Kate said with a grin as she picked up the instrument. 'Kate Phillips of Darfield Animal Care speaking.' She looked as if it was hard to focus on reality and not what had gone on in here moments ago.

Finn grinned as he waited for the call to finish.

'Got a cat that needs some stitches in a paw coming in,' Kate told him when she put the phone down. 'It's one way to get back on track.'

'I can stay around to help with the cat if you want,' he said, not ready to leave her.

Kate shook her head firmly. 'I'll be fine, thanks.'

'You want me to go.'

'I think it's best, don't you? I mean, what happened was awesome, but work is intervening and I don't want to mix the two.'

She was right, but a little gremlin made him say, 'Not really.'

Taken aback, Kate stared at him. 'We're meant to only be friends.'

'I know, but seems there's more to this than either of us expected. We've kind of blown that theory.' When she didn't say anything he stepped closer and brushed a kiss over her lips. 'See you tomorrow.'

And hard as it was, he did walk away. Because Kate was right. They were becoming friends, not friends with benefits. Except they'd blown that out of the water and needed to cool down and see what they really wanted next.

As he drove back to the flat he thought about moving in with Kate if he couldn't find anywhere else. Only a few hours ago he'd rung the rental agencies and received the same answer—nothing available in the district. So far the choices were: going into the city where there were rentals available, or staying with Kate for as long as it took to find what he required.

Moving to the city would be a drag when he worked out here. But sharing a house with Kate would be tricky. Exciting, sure, but despite that incredible sex he was still afraid of his heart being broken again. Because she had just got in deeper than ever and he still wasn't ready. Sharing her house would mean they'd more than likely carry on with what they'd started today. While he'd be on tenterhooks all the time, waiting for the crash, the damaged heart. Basically the whole nightmare he was determined never to face again.

So staying with Kate looked nigh on impossible. He wanted to kiss her, make love to her, again. Admit it, he wanted to get to know her better. To share day-to-day occurrences with her. Which meant setting himself up to be vulnerable.

Silly man. That could not happen. She was so beautiful inside and out it wouldn't take much for her to have him in her hand to do with as she pleased. It would be impossible to resist her, which would be fine until he remembered he wasn't prepared for a life partner and pulled back. They'd need to spend all their time avoiding each other. Not comfortable at all. And not easy to do when sharing a kitchen and a lounge.

The alarm went off and Kate rolled over in bed with a sigh.

Finn knew how to kiss like the devil. He'd stirred her up even more when he'd made love to her. Her body hadn't stopped craving him ever since.

Damn it, Finn. How do you do this to me?

Try as she might to deny the afterglow of last night, it was impossible. It was also impossible to deny that Finn was waking her up in unexpected ways, which would only lead to trouble because the day would come when she'd have to expose her insecurities. She'd been lucky last night not to have exposed the scars. They hadn't turned on the lights as there'd been enough moonlight

coming through the window for them to carry
on as they'd started. But if he wanted more from
her, and she believed he might, she was ready
for a lot of things but not to show him her body
and have him stare at her as though she was the
ugliest thing he'd ever encountered.

Okay, an exaggeration, but she'd been hurt by
other men who hadn't been able to refrain from
saying the first thing that had popped into their
miserable minds. She had to remember Finn
would be protecting himself after his previous
relationship.

The alarm repeated its loud drumming. Five
minutes gone already, spent thinking about the
one person she shouldn't be. Finn Anderson had
a lot to answer for.

After a shower she dressed in jeans and a blue
tee shirt before scoffing down tea and toast. She
fed her dogs, and took them for a walk along the
street as Rusty had little difficulty with his damaged leg now. After that she went in to work. The
clinic only opened in the morning on Saturdays
but no doubt she'd be called in some time over
the afternoon. Mark said he'd take any calls once
the barbecue was under way. She was grateful
for his generous offer, though it didn't seem fair
on his wife and kids. Then again, she'd covered
for him three weekends ago when he'd had a
family party to attend out of town.

'Hey, Di, I got your list of who's coming and what they're all bringing this afternoon, thanks.' They'd opened the door and already people were arriving with their pets. 'Doesn't seem like there's much for me to do.' She'd hit the grocery store after work to get snacks and mixes for drinks, plus some frozen desserts.

'You know how it works.' Di laughed as she brought their first dog of the morning into the treatment room with its owner. 'Tipsy's due for a parvo jab.'

Yes, thought Kate, she knew how everyone always brought more than enough for an army to eat, and the men shared the cooking on the barbecue while the women watched out for the kids and enjoyed a drink. It was always a good way for everyone to relax together and seemed to keep the usual staff grizzles at bay. This would be the first one Finn attended, and she was certain he'd fit right in. He did with everything else.

'Too well,' Kate decided as she watched him turning steaks on the barbecue, beer in hand, and laughing with the guys.

'He gets on with everyone, doesn't he?' Di was watching Finn too. 'Has he found anywhere to live yet?'

'Not yet. He's got another week left before he has to get out of the place he's renting.' By then hopefully he'd have found something because after last night she couldn't see them getting along comfortably while sharing her home unless they continued having a fling, something she was trying not to think about. 'I didn't realise how difficult it was finding rental properties out this way.'

'There aren't that many places to rent and it's harder in summer for some reason. I have heard that some townies think living out here will be wonderful, then along comes winter and they suddenly miss the lights of the city and the shorter drive home in the dark after work.' Di shrugged. 'I don't think Finn's one of those.'

'Definitely not.' He'd talked about living in Scotland and the freezing winters and lack of people around in the worst times, but not once had he said he hadn't enjoyed it. Except for the cold, he'd seemed to love his time there.

'I think it would be cool if he moved in with you.' Di gave her a wink. 'Who knows what might come of that?'

'Nothing,' she snapped. When Di grinned, Kate said, 'It can't. We work together.' Hell, even she was getting tired of that excuse. Especially after last night.

'So what? Mark and Dorothy worked together and look how that worked out.'

'They do have a great marriage.' Kate sighed.

'But they're them and I'm not looking for a partner at the moment.' Something else that was getting tiring.

'Kate, you got a minute?' Finn was walking across the lawn in her direction, wearing his serious face.

Her heart sank. This felt wrong. As if he was about to tip her world upside down. Hadn't he already done that? And didn't she feel a teeny bit excited about everything? 'Sure.'

'I'll start putting the salads out,' Di said and left her with Finn.

'What's up?' Her heart rate was rising rapidly. They couldn't live together in the same house. She needed to put space between them. Needed to remember how men had treated her in the past.

'This is not what I thought I'd be asking of you this soon, if at all. Especially now that we've got closer.' He drew a breath. 'Can I take you up on your offer?'

Her head spun. What to do? She had made the offer, but that was before they'd had sex.

'It's all right. I'll move to the city.'

'No, you won't.' She couldn't say no, could she? She'd have to find a way to protect her heart but she couldn't make him leave the district when he worked here. Besides, everyone would think she wasn't being nice when she'd already said it was fine. 'Come inside and I'll show you around.' If only they hadn't had sex. But they had, and now they had to get past it if Finn was going to share her home. Or they could go crazy and have lots of sex so she could get this need out of her system.

'I know this isn't what you wanted, but I've run out of options. It's a week sooner than I have to move but all the agencies say it's not looking hopeful. Also the owner hassles me every day to get out so he can do the few maintenance jobs that are part of the sale agreement, and, to be honest, I've had enough of him always asking if I've found somewhere to live.' Finn sounded flat, which was unlike him.

Turning to him, she said, 'It's all right. We'll make it work. I like having someone in the house. It gets a bit too quiet at times. That is, except when the dogs are super energetic. Though their conversation skills need some work.'

Finn smiled tightly. 'You're a champ. I know last night has made things awkward, but we're grown-ups, we can move on from that.'

'True.' Her heart plummeted. He was right. Only thing was, she would love some more of those kisses and the sex that had followed. Spinning around, she headed for the bedroom that was to become Finn's. 'Have you got your own furniture?'

Stepping into the room, Finn looked around. 'Not a thing. The last place came furnished.'

'No problem. The bedroom has everything you need.'

'You've got it all sorted, haven't you?'

'I try to be organised.' Didn't always work out but still. 'When were you thinking of moving in?'

'Tomorrow. If that's all right with you. Otherwise it'll have to be after work one night.'

She winced. Nothing like no time to get prepared, but then she probably never would be so might as well get it over and done. Once Finn was here, she'd be able to stop wondering how she'd cope, and get on with doing whatever it took. 'I'll get you the keys so you can bring your gear around any time you like. I'm on call tomorrow so might not be around all the time.'

Back in the kitchen she looked outside. Everyone was gathered around her large wooden table, filling plates with food. 'Looks like they're starting without us.'

'Come on. Let's join them and I'll get the keys before I go home.'

'If you forget, there's a spare back-door key hanging on the back of Rusty's kennel. He'll probably give it to you.' Rusty had followed him around the yard from the moment he'd turned up for the barbecue. 'He obviously doesn't blame you for his injured leg.'

'He seems fine now, doesn't he? I know he isn't running or going for long walks, but nor is he limping.'

Her boy was doing fine. 'Thanks to you.'

'I'll take that.' His smile lightened her further.

If a smile did that, how was she going to manage to stay on track with him living in the house? It might prove very interesting over the coming weeks. Or months? How long would Finn end up living here? He hadn't even unpacked a bag yet and she was wondering that? Time to get out amongst everyone and put some space between them. But as she stepped off the deck to join her friends, her hand touched her abdomen, reminding her why she got in such a pickle when it came to letting a man into her life. But Finn was only renting a bedroom, not moving into her bed—or her heart.

At the table, she grabbed a plate and concentrated on placing steak and salads and potatoes on it. Her head was spinning. Her heart was not getting involved. It couldn't be. Too risky. Somehow she felt if she truly started falling for Finn, she wouldn't be able to stop. It would hurt worse than ever when he walked away.

What if he didn't?

What?

Why wouldn't he? The man she'd loved so much that she'd believed they'd be together for ever had, so why would she expect another one to stay with her? But Hamish had already stopped loving her when she had been attacked by the stingers, and had only stayed with her afterwards because he'd felt guilty about her coming into the water to save him when he'd had an epileptic fit. 'I can't do this any more.' Yes, those words still reverberated around her head at times. That was when she'd finally learned he'd taken her to North Queensland for a holiday in the hope of finding he could still love her, and not because they had been so in love that he'd had to spend time away with her in an awesome location. His secretary had won in the end.

'You all right?' Finn asked quietly beside her. 'You've gone awfully pale.'

Glancing at him, she felt a tight squeeze in her chest. No, she wasn't all right. This man had also said something very similar last year. The words still reverberated around her head at awkward moments. *I'm sorry. I can't do this.* Even though his words weren't backed up with the same unbelievable truth that she was no longer loved by her man, they had the capacity to upset her all over again. Best to keep that to herself. 'I'm good. Need to eat some food, that's all.'

He stared at her in disbelief. 'I can move into the city,' he reiterated.

She was letting Finn down. Or he thought she was. 'No. Really, no. You're staying here.' Strange how that felt the right thing to say when her head and heart were in disagreement with each other. 'I mean it. In fact, let's let everyone know now.' Then there'd be no backing out on her part.

'Only if you are absolutely certain, Kate. I don't want to upset you.'

'Didn't I just say that I am certain?' He could see through her. Surely he had his own doubts about what he was about to do? If he didn't, then she'd read him wrong.

'Yes, you did. Okay, ready for this?' he asked through one of his gorgeous smiles.

'Totally.' She put her plate down and tapped the side of a glass with her fork. 'Listen up, everyone. Finn's moving into my spare bedroom tomorrow as it seems there're no rentals available around Darfield at the moment.'

'Need a hand moving your gear?' Mark asked.

Finn grimaced. 'What I've got goes in the back of the car just fine. I haven't been back in the country long enough to amass lots of furniture or anything else, but thanks for the offer.'

'Kate's got more than enough of everything inside this house,' Peter said.

'Make me sound like a kleptomaniac, why don't you?' Kate retorted. 'But I wouldn't mind if some of you did come tomorrow and help me move some furniture out to the storage shed.' She had been wanting for a while to have a bit of a clean-out but needed some manpower to lift the furniture.

'Count me in,' Peter said.

'And me,' Mark added. 'What time?'

'Sort it with Finn so he can have help lifting his cases out of his vehicle.' She tried to laugh as she picked up her plate. Not easy when she was suddenly in a flurry of nerves about Finn coming to live with her. 'Come on, everyone. Let's enjoy dinner.'

So I can pretend everything's all right and I am not worrying about how to deal with that sexy man wandering around my house at all hours.

She took her plate and sat down next to Sheree. 'How're you getting on with the wedding plans?' Their daughter was getting married in three months and Sheree had taken over organising everything.

'Not bad.'

As Sheree filled her in on everything, Kate tried to settle the nerves tightening her. It was official. Finn was going to be living with her. Everyone had accepted it as though it was an everyday occurrence. Which it probably was, even for her. She had been thinking about finding a new housemate, just hadn't expected to feel so disorientated by the one she'd got.

She looked around, her gaze coming to rest on Finn sitting with Mark and Campbell, Di's partner, chatting away as if he didn't have a worry in the world. Why would he? His housing problem had been solved. He was fitting in with everyone very well. He was back home for good. But there were times when she felt he struggled with feeling at ease with his life. Obviously he hadn't got over what his fiancée had done to him and was constantly on guard. He probably had as many trust issues as she did, if not more.

Sheree nudged her. 'He's quite a catch, isn't he?'

Kate swallowed as her face warmed. Why was everyone trying to pair her up with someone? Mentioning Finn as though it were the ideal answer to her problem? 'Good-looking for sure.'

'That's not what I meant.'

'No, I surmised it wasn't.'

'Kate, I know you've been hurt in the past so I get that you're not in a hurry to find a man to share your life with, but Finn might be worth taking a second look at.'

Here we go again.

Why couldn't her friends leave her to sort out

her life herself? Because she hadn't done a good job so far? Probably.

'I hear you, but I'll make the decisions about my private life, thanks, Sheree,' she said with a smile. No way did she want to upset her friend, but neither did she need any interference over how she conducted her life.

Sheree laughed. 'Just giving you the heads up. Now I'll shut up.'

'Thank goodness for that,' Kate said before realising she was still watching Finn. Yep, he was definitely doing her head in, and he hadn't moved in yet.

CHAPTER SEVEN

'KATE, WE HAVEN'T discussed the rent,' Finn said the next morning, dumping his three cases in what was to be his bedroom. Over the hall from Kate's. Too damned close by far, but then it could be at the end of the street and it would be too close. How the hell was he ever going to get any sleep knowing Kate was so near to him?

When she gave him the figure, he said, 'That can't be right. It's way too low.' He wasn't here for charity.

Kate looked a little flummoxed. 'It's all I ask for.'

He tried for light-hearted. 'I get it. I do all the housework, cook every meal and mow the lawns.'

'Bang on.' Her smile was tired, but at least it was a smile.

'Kate, it's still not too late to change the plan.' Though he'd be gutted if she changed her mind now. He'd spent a lot of the night thinking about it and knew it was the best option as long as Friday night didn't get in the way. There'd been a lot of reminiscing about that too, and how Kate had felt in his arms and how hot and wonderful her body had been as they'd made love. Getting to know Kate better had to be a good thing because deep down he felt something soft and caring for her. Something like love, though not really love. Because love was not allowed. Too dangerous for his heart.

Snap. No more smile. 'We are not going over this again. We've made an agreement and we're sticking to it. Anyway, it's too late. If you found something in the city you wouldn't be moving in today. You'd have to go shopping for furniture and everything else required to live in a house.' Turning her back on him, she strode inside, leaving him to deal with his gear.

'Fair enough,' he called after her, not sure if she'd heard.

A car turned into the driveway. He wasn't alone. Peter and Mark were here to help store whatever Kate wanted out of the house. They'd get on with the job and then he'd go give the flat one last tidy up, leaving nothing for the owner to complain about, and then come back to settle into his new abode. Hopefully he'd then get to spend time with Kate and talk about anything but the fact she didn't seem happy for him to be here.

Though it might be best to get over that hurdle sooner rather than later so they could move on more comfortably.

'Finn.' Kate was back, this time with both dogs at her side, as if they were bargaining chips or something.

'Aye?' He put out a hand to Sam and got a short nudge with his nose.

Kate's smile was firmer this time. The kind that always knocked on his heart. 'When you're finished putting my things in the shed, bring the others in for a coffee and left-over cake from the barbecue.'

Was this her way of apologising for being abrupt? She didn't owe him one, but he'd let it go as he didn't want to cause any more tension between them. 'Give us twenty minutes. There's not a lot to do.' She'd already pointed out what she wanted removed from the rooms.

'I've still got to give the flat keys back,' Finn told Kate an hour later when the guys had left. 'Do a bit of vacuuming.'

'I'll come and give you a hand,' she told him.

'That's not necessary.'

'Maybe, but I'd like to.'

He wouldn't argue. This was a way to get over the hurdle between them. 'Then let's get it done.' It would make the job less boring having Kate doing some of the cleaning. Face it, Kate made everything less boring just by being around.

'I'll take my car in case I get called in to the clinic.'

'Come with me, and if that happens I'll go with you.' It seemed pointless to take two vehicles to West Melton. 'Want me to put the dogs in their kennels?'

'They'll be fine in the yard. We won't be all day.'

But they were later than planned. When Finn pulled out of West Melton he noted Two Fat Possums, a bar slash café, in the row of shops, and made an instant decision. Pulling into the car park, he said, 'I'm starving. Let's have a late lunch.'

Spending time with Kate on neutral territory would be a way to quieten his busy mind and heart. He wasn't looking to ask a load of questions, but it would be good to clear the air by having a relaxed meal and light conversation. If that was possible.

'Good idea.' Kate was out of the ute in a blink, smoothing down her shirt and brushing her hair back behind her ears.

She looked good enough to eat. Yep, he was starving for more than food. Now he'd become her housemate it was going to be harder not to follow up on those feelings, especially as his body knew hers a little better now. 'My shout.'

Her hair swished back and forth across her shoulders. 'I owe you for operating on Rusty.'

'You don't, but I'm not going to waste time arguing.' There'd be other opportunities to take her out for a meal. 'Have you been here before?'

'A couple of times. The food's great and there's great seating outside in a covered courtyard.'

'Not possum meat, I hope.'

'What else would they have?' She laughed, a deep, sexy sound that had him longing for her. Damn it, he had to get beyond these feelings or he'd never get a proper night's sleep while he lived in her home.

He went with seafood pizza even though Kate had been joking with him about possum meat.

'You don't trust me?' She grinned.

'Nope.' He could fall into that grin and not come up for air for a long time. 'I do enjoy a good pizza though. Like a beer? Or a wine?'

'I'll have a soda since I'm on call. What about you?' She had her cash card in her hand. Probably didn't trust him not to take over and pay for lunch.

'Same.' He went to find them a table in the outdoor area. She was right. It was shaded but warm, and the tables were spaced so that he didn't feel as if they'd be sitting so close to the next table that conversation would be impossible.

Kate placed the order number in its holder on the table, along with two sodas on mats. Sitting on the stool, she glanced around. 'I haven't been here for a while.'

'Where did you live before moving to Darfield?'

'After Hamish and I broke up I flatted in Lincoln while I saved to buy a house. I wanted something to call my own. It gave me security and confidence over what I chose to do.'

So her ex had made it hard for her to believe in herself. 'Running your own life, eh?'

She nodded. 'With no one to change the plan.'

'There's something secure in owning your own home.' One day he'd be able to do that again. Next time he'd make sure no one could take it away from him. Kate might not be the sort to do what Amelia had, but he would struggle to trust anyone that much again.

'There sure is.' Her soda was going down fast. 'I believed Hamish and I had that together. I know, that sounds trite, but that's how it was for me.'

'Nothing wrong with that. I felt that way about Amelia. My fiancée,' he added in case he hadn't mentioned her name when he'd told Kate about her.

'It puts the kibosh on trust, doesn't it?' Now there was a haunted look on Kate's face that twisted his gut.

'It sure does.' He wanted to say more but was worried he'd say something that'd upset her even further. Nor did he want to expose more of his distrust about relationships. Looking around, he saw the waitress approaching with their meals. 'Those look good.'

Kate settled further onto her stool, looking relieved. 'Sure do.'

They ate in silence until a young child at a table in the corner started crying and shoved his plate away. 'I don't like fish.'

'You did last week,' the man with him, presumably his dad, replied quietly.

'Did not.'

Kate smiled. 'The joys of parenthood, eh?'

'I wouldn't know,' Finn said quietly. When the truth came out, his heart had broken all over again.

'Would you like to be a dad one day?'

Absolutely. It would be wonderful. He filled his mouth with pizza. It wasn't happening.

Kate was looking at him with disappointment. She wanted to learn more about him. As he did about her. Okay, he'd do his best to open up a little and see where that went. But he sure as hell wasn't telling her how Amelia told him she was pregnant in an attempt to keep him with her until she found someone else to give her the life comforts and money she craved.

'I'd love to have a family to call my own. Little horrors running around my home and making me laugh and cry and adore them to bits.' How was that for a genuine answer? More than he usually put out there. 'I'm just not ready yet.' Not likely to ever be, but that was for him to know.

A glimmer of a smile appeared. 'Little horrors, eh? Dad used to call us those when we were very young. Usually followed up with an ice cream.'

'Must be a generational thing, because it was the same in our home growing up.' Something they had in common, apart from their careers, and broken hearts. 'Does that mean you'd like a family one day too?'

'Definitely.' Kate forked chips into her mouth.

Okay, he got it. Ask no more. For now. 'You've had a quiet day so far for being on call.'

Swallowing, Kate shook her head at him. 'Thanks. Bet I get something now.'

'Yeah, the moment the words left my mouth I knew I'd set you up.'

'That's how it works.' Taking a sip of her drink, she said, 'You seem happy to have moved out of that flat.'

'Now that I have, I am. I was never overly

happy with the place, a bit too cramped, but it was somewhere to put my head down at night while I got organised with what I want long term. Unfortunately time ran out too soon.' He'd got into the groove of saving every dollar or pound he earned, first to pay off debts incurred by Amelia and then to build up some funds so he could buy a house or set up a vet practice in the near future.

Though that second option didn't seem as important now, since working at Darfield Animal Care was ticking all the boxes for him. It was a good practice with excellent vets, and the staff were friendly and focused. A glance at Kate reminded him who his favourite colleague was. Had he made a mistake moving in with Kate? Especially after their hot night at the clinic? Too late. Whatever the answer, he had already moved in. He'd keep looking for somewhere else in case this didn't work.

'I was a bit surprised when I saw the flat. It doesn't appear to have had any maintenance for quite a while.'

'Never, if you ask me. I don't think there's a lot of spare cash in that household. But I couldn't turn it down when I'd taken weeks to find somewhere to rent.' Finn ate the last piece of pizza and pushed his plate aside. 'That was perfect.'

Kate nodded in agreement. 'It's not a bad place for casual meals. I—'

Her phone rang.

Glancing at the screen, she shrugged. 'Guess it had been too good to be true. Hello, this is Kate Phillips from Darfield Animal Care. How can I help you?'

Finn drained his glass. They were on the move. No such thing as a second round and more conversation about themselves. That had to be good, though he did like getting to know Kate. She was lovely, and while she had issues from the past she was getting on with her life. She had a job she seemed to love, and had bought her own home, had two dogs as well. He could learn from her. Was she content? Or did she get lonely at times? As he did after a long day at work and going home to an empty place to cook a meal with no one to share it with? At least that would be different for the coming weeks until he found a permanent place to rent.

Kate slid her phone into her pocket and stood up. 'I need to go to the clinic. A poodle has eaten her owner's pills. Quite a list of them, by the sounds of it.'

'No time to waste, then.'

Wish I'd brought my car, Kate thought as Finn drove them back to Darfield. She could do with a break from him. He was too much. Too sexy, too good-looking, too desirable. He'd only moved in today and she was already in a pickle.

'Want a hand with the poodle?' he asked.

'No, I'll be fine. Drop me off and head home.' Having him in the same space at the clinic was the last thing she needed right now. 'I'll walk back after I'm done.' Lunch at the Two Fat Possums had been great. They'd relaxed together, talked a bit more about themselves, but she could only take so much Finn air before her body started to get wound up and need release— with Finn. They needed to have a big argument over something so she'd have an excuse to ignore him.

Ha! She laughed. She really did come up with some mad ideas at times. All to protect herself from getting hurt.

'What's funny?'

'I have no idea.' It was the truth. It wasn't funny that she had to think of ways to keep Finn at arm's length. 'Just a random thing.'

'I see.'

Bet he didn't. Instead he'd probably be thinking she was a fruit loop. Which might have him looking harder for somewhere else to live. Then she'd be disappointed about that. No winning for Finn. Or her.

Yet when she got home after treating the poodle and there was no sign of Finn or his vehicle, she had to remind herself they weren't a couple and that he'd be coming and going as he pleased while staying with her.

A note sat on the bench.

Gone to see Mum and Dad, having dinner with them. Finn.

See? They were housemates. 'Okay, boys, let's go for a walk.' Grabbing the leads, she headed down the drive with her dogs running around her excitedly. Once they were clipped onto their leads, she opened the gate and turned towards the main road.

During weekends Darfield was quiet apart from the supermarket and takeaway outlets. The majority of retail properties were about farming equipment and supplies, and other outdoor requirements. As they walked past the bakery Kate sniffed the air and caught a whiff of something delicious she couldn't recognise. On the job late, by the smell of it.

Despite the burger and chips she'd had earlier, her stomach did a flip. Seemed it was hungry again. Around the corner she stopped at the Indian takeaway and ordered lamb korma for one, then continued walking her dogs along to the park where teenage boys were skating on the rink, making a racket as they did spins and flips.

Finally back at home she fed Rusty and Sam,

then sat down in front of the TV with the korma to watch a crime programme. The house felt eerily quiet. The dogs lay in their beds as per normal. No traffic was going along the street. All perfectly usual and yet it seemed different. Because Finn would be here later and she couldn't wait to see him, to find out how they'd get along with this arrangement. Yes, she was totally out of sorts. He had got to her in lots of ways, the hardest to accept was that she was starting to think more of him than just a friend.

Whenever they'd worked together on a patient they'd been a team. No difficulties over who did what, or how either of them did a procedure. They just got on with what was required. She was always aware of him whenever he was near and that hadn't happened with other men she'd known since Hamish. He was continually in her head space, winding her up with an image of his to-die-for smile. As for his love-making—that was something else. Blood-heating, heart-pounding, toe-tingling kisses that had her yearning for more. A lot more.

Except for her there was one huge wall in the way of getting close and intimate. Her scars. Shoving her plate aside, she stood up and went to the bathroom where she lifted her tee shirt and lowered her jeans. The scars no longer horrified her. She was used to them. The problem lay in what men had said about them. Running her fingers over her skin, she stared at herself. Her skin wasn't rough. Enough time had gone by for the scars to soften. Unfortunately they hadn't lost much of the angry reddish pink colour, and that was what seemed to draw the attention of the men she'd tried to be intimate with.

Looking up, she studied her face. Her skin was perfect, nothing marring the light tanned shade. Her eyes were big and, yes, beautiful. Her lips were naturally full and sexy. But none of that mattered. It was what was on the inside that counted. When she was growing up, her parents had made certain she understood that, and mostly she'd agreed, though there had been a time in her teens when she'd got a bit too big for her boots and used her beauty to get what she wanted. It hadn't lasted long. She'd over-heard two boys saying they wanted to get into her pants and see if the rest of her was as good, and from then on she'd made sure any guy she spent time with liked her for who she was, not only her face.

What would Finn think if he got to see her naked? Would he make awful comments like those she'd heard before? She couldn't see him doing that, but she could imagine him shudder-ing and turning away without a word—which was as horrific as what others had voiced. Guess she'd never know what his reaction would be because he wasn't going to see her without clothes on. So, end any thoughts about getting closer. They had to remain friends, no more, and hopefully no less.

Pulling her clothes straight, she went back to finish her dinner, only the korma didn't taste as appetising as it had a few minutes earlier.

It was nearly ten when the programme finished. Kate took the dogs out for a pee then let them back in to go to their beds. Leaving the outside light on, she had a quick shower and got into her bed with the crime story she was currently reading. When Finn got home she turned the bedside light off and snuggled down under the lightweight duvet, pretending all was well in her head.

Finn walking through the house and down the hall to his bedroom opposite hers said all was not quite as good as she'd like it. Finn was the man waking her up from what felt like a long sleep. It had been kind of like that over the months since she'd decided no more dating after the last man walked away. Not only was she waking up, but she was beginning to hope. She was already feeling a little bit in love with Finn, though not so much that she couldn't back away, and it was as though a whole new world was opening up. An exciting world where love was guaranteed, where children were included, and nobody gave her grief over something she couldn't change.

Dream on.

Early the next morning Finn parked outside the joint bakery café where they made the best ever breakfasts and right now he was starving. He hadn't slept well. The bed was perfect: firm yet soft. The house had been quiet except whenever the dogs did a lap of the hall, obviously making sure Mum was still there. But it was the goings-on in his head that had kept sleep at bay.

In other words, Kate. This morning he hadn't been ready to chat over toast as though everything were all right so here he was, about to order breakfast and then go in to work where he'd see Kate at the weekly meeting.

Kate was ruling him. Not that she'd be aware of it. He hoped not anyway. How had he got to this point when he was so determined never to fall in love again? Did he love Kate? No, he did not. But it felt as though he was well on the way. Living with her was making it difficult to keep the lid on his emotions.

'What would you like, Finn?' the woman behind the counter asked.

He recognised her as the owner of a herd of cows he'd vaccinated a couple of weeks ago. 'Bacon and eggs with hash browns, thanks,

Heather. Plus a large long black double shot.'
He desperately needed caffeine to wake him up
fully.

'Coming right up.'

He had picked a quiet moment. No truckies
in sight and too early for mothers stopping in
for their morning fix after dropping the kids
off at school.

'Got a lot on today?' Heather asked as the coffee machine hissed.

'I'm heading out to Rangiora later in the
morning to look at some sheep with facial ec-
zema.'

'Nice.'

'All part of the job.' He grinned, finally letting
go some of the tightness gripping him.

'You can have it.' Heather placed a large mug
in front of him. 'Breakfast won't be long.'

'No hurry.' Once he'd eaten he'd still be early
arriving at the clinic and no doubt Kate would
already be there. She seemed to like to get her
day sorted before everyone else turned up. He
hadn't heard her moving around the house when
he'd left. Keeping low until he'd gone? His laugh
was taut. They did need to get along normally
or the days when he was in the clinic would be
tough along with the evenings at the house.

'Morning, Finn. You left early.' Kate smiled

warmly as he strode into the office forty-five minutes later.

'Morning. I was too late leaving Mum and Dad's last night to stop at the supermarket and get some groceries so I went to the bakery for breakfast.' That was true. 'I'm sure you wouldn't have minded if I helped myself to whatever was in the pantry or fridge, but I was starving and a big breakfast did the trick.'

'Your mum didn't feed you enough?' she asked.

'More than, but my appetite seems out of hand lately. Too much time spent walking around farms maybe?'

Hadn't he done that in Scotland? 'Better than being inside all day.' Her gaze cruised his body, heating him when that was the last thing he needed right now. Or any time.

What? He'd gone off sex? With a woman who had the ability to pull him in close emotionally? Absolutely. 'You'd like to be outdoors on the job?' So far she'd always said she preferred the domestic side to the work they did.

Her thick plait swished across her back when she shook her head. 'Not really. Winter can be harsh, and anyway I prefer dogs and cats to cows and bulls. Sheep are all right, but they're so dumb.'

'You want intelligent animals to treat?'

'If I have to talk to them when I'm checking them out, then of course I do.' She sounded serious but there was a mischievous gleam in her eyes. Lightening up?

The front door crashed open. 'Finn, give me a hand, will you?' Mark called. 'I've got an Alsatian in the back of my car that's been hit by a truck. Not looking good.'

Kate leapt to her feet. 'What can I do?'

'Open the operating room and turn on some lights,' Mark yelled, his voice full of dread.

'That bad?' Finn was tight behind him when he reached the back door of his SUV.

'Yep. Toby belongs to my neighbour. One of their kids left the gate open when she set off for school.'

The dog barely responded to being lifted out of the vehicle and carried inside between them. As soon as Toby was laid on the table Finn swung the X-ray machine above him. 'We'll start with finding out the real damage.'

'Broken back leg for a start,' Mark replied as he arranged the dog in a way that they could get a clear picture of his organs and ribs.

'Stand back,' Finn warned as soon as Mark was ready.

The X-rays showed three fractured ribs with both lungs perforated. Blood was oozing from

Toby's mouth and his breathing was getting more laboured by the minute.

'What do you think?' Finn asked Mark.

'His owner said to do all I could to save him.'

'I'll help you with the surgery if you'd like.'

Mark's nod was abrupt. 'Thanks.'

'You two carry on here and don't worry about the meeting.' Kate spoke up behind them, giving Finn a fright. He'd forgotten all about her while dealing with Toby. 'Unless you want me to take your place, Finn?'

'No, I'm good here.'

'I know, but you have got a lot on today.' Her voice was tight, as though she'd prefer he didn't do this. She was in charge of the domestic side of the business after all.

But she had other things to do that he couldn't. Glancing her way, he found her watching him closely. 'I'll manage. Toby needs help now, and you've got a meeting to run.' It was true. Peter wasn't coming in this morning and it wasn't *his* place to run the meeting.

'Fine.' She left the room in a hurry.

So much for getting along. That had gone down the drain the moment an emergency cropped up. Turning to Mark, he asked, 'Want me to administer the anaesthetic?'

'You do that and I'll get ready to open Toby up. Hopefully we're not too late. His breathing doesn't appear to have altered much in the last few minutes.'

That had to be because it was already about as slow as it could be without actually stopping. Finn kept that to himself. Mark would be fully aware of the situation.

Much later, Finn tossed his gloves in the bin with relief. 'We did it.'

Mark high-fived him. 'We did. Thanks for your help.'

'Kate would've done the same,' he said.

'I know. But she's got a lot on today with Peter being away and the operating list chock-full. We don't usually do surgical bookings on Monday but there's been so many people wanting to bring their pets in for one thing or another we had to do an extra list.'

She hadn't mentioned that to him but then she didn't have to, he supposed. 'I'm going to grab a coffee and head out to Rangiora.' He wasn't hanging around where he wasn't needed. He and Kate would have enough time together tonight when they were at home.

'How did it go with the extra op list?' Finn asked Kate as he cleared the table after dinner.

'All good.' Peter had stunned her when he'd phoned early to ask her to step in for him as he had to take Sheree to the doctor. The man never stepped away from work no matter what arose in his private life. She'd phoned before heading home only to be told it was a false alarm and that Sheree was fine.

'I'd have been shocked if it wasn't.'

'What?' She stared at Finn, completely at a loss as to what he was talking about.

'Ah, hello, Kate. I mentioned the surgical list.'

She huffed out a breath. 'Sorry. I was miles away.'

His face tightened. 'So I see.'

'Finn, stop it. I was thinking about something else, that's all. Nothing to get your knickers in a twist about, okay?' Even to her, she sounded a bit harsh. 'Sorry again. I take that back. It's been a busy day.'

'It must've been, because I don't wear knickers. Not lacy G-strings, anyway.' His smile was tentative, as if he expected her to lose her cool again.

'You're saying you go commando?' Where the hell did that come from? This was Finn, the man she was trying to remain immune to, and she'd asked if he went without underwear? Bloody hell. She was in deep trouble if nonsense like that poured from her mouth whenever she wasn't being careful around him.

'No comment.' His smile was cheeky and not

giving anything away as he wiped the bench and set the dishwasher to start.

The second night into the rental agreement and this was happening. Kate walked around Finn to get the kettle and filled it to make tea. Anything to keep busy and quieten her overactive mind. Holding a mug in both hands would keep them out of trouble. 'Want tea or coffee?'

'No, thanks. I'm going to watch something on TV. If that's all right with you,' he added sharply.

'Why wouldn't it be?' She spun around to face him, her hip bumping into him. She reached out to steady herself and came up against his chest.

Her hands were instantly encased in Finn's and she was being drawn closer to his sensational body. Raising her head, she found him watching her with a longing that undid all her resolve to remain cautious. 'Finn,' she croaked over a suddenly dry tongue.

Beautiful suck-me-in brown eyes locked on him. 'Finn,' she whispered.

His breathing stopped. Just like that she had him in the palm of her hand. 'Kate,' he whispered back. But then that was what he'd wanted as he drew her in against his body. Wrapping his arms around her, he leaned back to look at her, to absorb her beauty and heat and sexiness. Instantly he was tight, so damned tight he ached for Kate. She was so gorgeous it was impossible to ignore these sensual feelings she engendered within him.

Before he could say anything more, her mouth was covering his, kissing him as though she'd been wanting this for ever. He knew how that felt, because he'd been longing for Kate from the moment he saw her when he walked into the clinic on his first morning working there. Of course he'd denied it, but it was true. Had been all along. And having sex with her the other night had not dulled the need one little bit. Now he was returning her kiss like a starved man. Which he was. Starved for love and sex and being part of someone's life.

Damn, she tasted wonderful. Felt even more wonderful. Her body was soft and strong, hot and warm, demanding and giving. He leaned in closer, held her tighter, and continued kissing her while losing all thought about anything but Kate.

Until she slid her mouth away and looked directly at him.

His heart sank. She was bailing.

'Your room or mine?'

Did he just hear right? 'Yours.' His bed wasn't as big as hers. Yes, he had seen inside her bedroom to know it was very feminine and the bed ever so welcoming with its big, soft eiderdown.

His hand was in Kate's and he was being

pulled down the hall into her room and then they were on the bed, back to kissing while their hands began exploring each other.

Then Kate stopped.

'What's up?' Apart from his erection.

She got off the bed and closed the curtains. Returning to the bed, she lifted the cover. 'Let's get underneath this. I'm a bit cold.'

'Sure.' Though every part of him was on fire, he'd agree to anything right this moment.

Then they were under the cover, legs entwined, hands and mouths busy, and he had no idea whether it was hot or cold. Just damned sexy. 'Kate, you're beautiful,' he murmured as he kissed his way down between her breasts.

She stilled, her mouth paused on his neck.

What had he said wrong? She *was* beautiful.

Then her tongue slid over his belly button and she relaxed. So did he. So much so she drove him to the peak with her tongue, licking, touching, bringing him to the brink.

'Slow down,' he groaned and lifted her over him so he could touch her and keep her from driving him insane with need. Then he touched her moist sex and knew little after that, other than when Kate climaxed she cried his name on a husky tongue and tightened around him as if she'd never let go. He drove deep inside her again and again until he couldn't hold back any longer and let go to the heat and need expanding throughout him. 'Oh, Kate, sweetheart, you are beautiful.'

Why did she shiver when he said that?

The next day at work Kate wondered if Finn was avoiding her as she didn't see him once at the clinic. He did have a busy schedule but he usually came in at the end of the day to top up whatever drugs or equipment he might've used. Was he having second thoughts about where their *friendship* was heading?

Please not that. So far their lovemaking had been beyond amazing. There'd been a moment when she'd nearly freaked out last night when she'd realised Finn would be able to see the scars if she didn't darken the room. Pulling the curtains had made all the difference and relaxed her to continue having a wonderful time. Later, when they had been lying curled up together, she'd kept a tight hold on the duvet for fear it might fall away, and when Finn had got out of bed saying he was going to his room the relief had been quick to appear. As much as spending all night together appealed, she wasn't ready for him to see her scars.

Until now she'd always forewarned the few men she'd slept with but she couldn't bring herself to do that with Finn. She liked him too much.

To watch him walk away would be harder than ever to cope with. He was special. Of course it would happen. It always did, but first she wanted as much time with Finn as she could get. Which might be seen to not being honest with him. She shivered at that thought. She was always honest. But her heart was in danger here, and that came first. Though she was risking it by having so much time with Finn, she still worried he might already be changing his mind about their fling.

When she got home that night Finn was already there and preparing steaks and salad for dinner.

She relaxed. She'd been overthinking everything, as per usual. 'Hey. You're busy.'

He threw her a grin. 'Hope you like baked potatoes.'

'I like anything I don't have to cook. How long before you want dinner? I've got to take the dogs for a walk.'

'I did that when I got in. They were champing at the bit to get out so I figured it was the least I could do to make them happy.'

'Talk about a perfect housemate.' He didn't have to do that. 'I'll have a shower, then.' At least he couldn't say he'd done that for her.

'I'll pour you a wine while you're doing that.'

'You haven't got a beer.'

'I was waiting for you to get home.'

There was a skip in her step as she made her way to the bathroom. Finn made her feel happy with his easy way of getting on doing things. Having him here was getting better by the day.

She'd be quick in the shower and join him to make the most of everything.

'How do you like your steak?' he called after her.

'Medium rare.' Was there any other way?

'Perfect.'

No, Finn was the perfect one around here. She glanced over her shoulder and found him watching her with a smile.

She'd bottle that and take it out whenever they weren't seeing eye to eye, which, hopefully, wasn't often.

CHAPTER EIGHT

SATURDAY DAWNED BRIGHT and sunny. The mountains in the background were clear. Kate had a bounce in her step as she walked the dogs around town before breakfast. Since Finn moved in it had become her new way of walking, happy and light. 'You're going to be home alone, guys. I'm going to the school fair.'

If they were lucky Charlotte would pop over, though she was going to the fair with her friends from school too. 'I'll take you for another walk when I get home,' she promised.

Back at home she headed for the shower. Finn had already left as he and Mark were setting up the vet clinic's stall at the school. It felt strange to be able to wander around the house in only her towel, something she hadn't done since he moved in. The sex was plentiful and breathtaking every time. So far she'd managed to keep her secret by staying under covers or not stripping off completely, but it couldn't last.

She knew that, and dreaded the moment she'd have to explain what had happened in Northern Queensland. The longer she put it off, the harder it would be when the time came to open up with Finn.

She threw bread into the toaster, and made some tea, then sat on a stool while she waited for the toast. The benches were spotless, and not a single cup or knife lay in the sink. Finn was very tidy, whether that was his norm or he was being ultra careful in her place, she didn't know. He usually cleaned up after himself at work, so this probably was his way. Which had her making sure she put anything she used straight into the dishwasher and not in the sink to rinse later. Talk about getting around on tiptoes whenever he was here.

The phone rang. 'Hi, Di. What's up?'

'Can you grab the box of toys from behind my desk on your way here? I forgot them in my hurry to get home last night.'

'No problem.' Time to get cracking. 'Are you already at the school?'

'Yes, and it's busy. Not only with stallholders setting up, but people with their pets are turning up already and the fair doesn't open for another hour.'

'That's enthusiasm for you. Right, I'm on my way.' As soon as she swapped the towel for jeans and a shirt, and got the dogs into the car, because now it did seem like a good idea to take them. They could do some socialising, which always went down well and also exhausted them so they slept for hours afterwards.

Finn saw Kate pull into the car park and went across to get the large box Di had asked her to pick up, wondering what sort of reception he'd get. Lately Kate sometimes seemed to run hot then cold as if she was hiding something from him, and that raised alarms. He couldn't bear the thought she wasn't completely honest with him.

Like he'd told her everything about his past?

His shoulders sagged. Good point.

'Morning. Oh, hello, you two.'

Her dogs were on the back seat of her car. He reached in and put leads on them. 'You're having a family day out, eh?'

Rusty bounded off the seat and around his legs, followed quickly by Sam. Finn kept hold of the leads in case they decided to do a runner. Though he doubted that would happen, they weren't used to being in crowds as far as he knew.

'I decided they might as well be here as at home alone. They're usually well behaved around people and other dogs.' Kate had the boot open and was lifting out a huge carton.

'That what Di wanted?'

'Yep.'

'Here, you take the dogs and I'll get that.'

'Cheers. It is heavy.' With the leads in one hand, she picked up a small backpack in the other. 'Some of the emergency equipment I've brought just in case something happens to an animal.'

'Or someone brings their pet for a check-up.' He laughed. Doing a lot of that lately. 'I hear we'll get a bit of that. Freebies all round.'

'Peter mentioned it to me too. He says that we'll pick up some new clients through it so it's no big deal.' Kate walked beside him, keeping the dogs on her other side, obviously happy too. 'I'm actually looking forward to the day. It's quite different from a normal work one.'

'Hi, Kate. Glad to see you've brought your dogs,' a woman of similar age to Kate called out as she came towards them.

'Hey, Lisa. You manning the dog training tent?'

'I am for the first couple of hours, then some more in the afternoon.'

'Lisa, this is Finn Anderson. He's working with us now.' Kate turned to him. 'Lisa and a friend run dog classes for all ages.'

'Hello, Lisa. Do you get a lot of attendees?' Dog training was big business, though whether that was the case out here in Darfield he had no idea.

'Unbelievable the number who come. It never used to be as busy in previous years, but I think more people are getting dogs and aren't always up to speed on training them.'

'I can believe that. There seem to be more dogs going through the clinic than I expected too.' He loved dogs and would get one once he was more settled. A sideways glance at Kate and longing gripped him. Spending the past week sharing her house had opened him up to the possibility that he could finally let go of the past that held him stuck in his belief he couldn't trust another woman to care about him as much as he cared for her. If only he didn't have this nagging sense she might be holding something back, that was.

Kate must've picked up on his thoughts because she gave him a quick glance followed by one of her devastating smiles. 'It's a fact—more people are taking dogs into their homes and lives than ever before.' Then she turned back to Lisa. 'Sorry, but we'd better keep moving. I've still got more cartons to get out of the car and set out in our stall.'

'Probably see you later on. We need to arrange a shopping trip,' Lisa told her.

'Good idea.'

'A shopping trip, eh?' Finn grinned.

'You bet. Not that I *need* any new clothes, but, hey, why not?' Kate looked a little embarrassed. Not used to spending up large?

Finn laughed. 'You're female. Clothes shopping is a given with most of you. And your friend Lisa is at the top of the list for that. Or are you better at it than her?'

'No comment.'

'In other words, yes.' Bet she didn't put her money into the gambling machines in the hope of buying something glamorous and expensive.

Down, boy. That was uncalled-for. You know Kate is careful with her money.

She had a mortgage to pay off, for one.

'The op shops like me when I get around to having a clean-out of my wardrobe.' Her face flushed redder. 'Not that I do it very often.'

'Hence the full wardrobe in the third bedroom.' He'd put his empty cases in that room the day he'd moved in and unpacked. They hadn't fitted into the wardrobe for all the clothes already taking up space.

'We balance each other out. You had three cases when you came to my place. They'd only be a start for me if I had to pack up and move.'

'Guess you're not shifting house any time soon, then.'

Her smile dipped. 'Probably not.'

And he'd thought she was more than happy with her house. Guess he didn't know her as well as he thought. On a positive note there was time ahead to improve on that. He did not want to go back to the awkward atmosphere that had hung over them some nights after work last week. They mightn't be getting into a relationship but they could do better than they'd managed so far. 'Good, I'm safe for a while.' He gave her a big smile to show he was not trying to be a pain in the backside.

'Just don't ask for more space for clothes, or you might have a problem.' Her smile had returned, though a little tentative. Then she changed the subject away from herself.

'If you do decide to get a puppy, then I strongly advise you using Lisa and Mary's training school. They have a very good reputation.'

'Good to know.' So Kate remembered him saying weeks ago that he would like to have a dog. What else did she remember? Hopefully he hadn't said anything too personal during the times they'd been together away from work. He did tend to keep a firm brake on what he told people about his past, but Kate had a way of getting under his radar without even trying.

Face it. That was something that he liked about her. Her ability to have him talking about things that he usually kept close to his chest made him feel he'd found a woman who wasn't all about herself and would not use him for her own purposes. But then he also hadn't met a woman since Amelia who brought him alive in a rush of heat and need so that he struggled with keeping her strictly in the 'friend with benefits' mode, which was worrying. Especially now, when he wondered if Kate was being as open as he'd first believed. He didn't want to move away but it might come to that to protect himself from falling in love and being hurt.

As they neared the clinic's stall, Rusty bounced around in a circle. 'Settle, boy. That's Di, yes, and you know you have to behave around her and everyone else.'

Di came over and rubbed both dogs on their heads. 'G'day, guys. Thanks for the box, Kate. We're nearly set up and there's a large space on the stand for all these toys to go.'

'I'll give you a hand with them,' Kate said. 'I'll just tie these two up somewhere out of everyone's way for now.'

Finn put the carton down and went to see how Mark was getting on with the table they'd use when anyone brought a pet in to be checked over. 'Looks like you're all sorted.'

'Took five attempts to get the legs straight, but hopefully it'll be good now. We can hang back and wait for the fun to start.'

'It'll probably be more waiting than doing.'

Kate's laughter came from behind him. 'From what everyone's told me we're in for a busy day. I thought I warned you.'

'I hoped you were exaggerating.'

Mark shook his head. 'Not likely. See, here we go and it's not even nine o'clock.'

Finn looked around to find a teenage girl carrying a cat basket walking towards them. 'Hi. I'm Finn, a vet. Does your cat need something?'

'Hi, Finn. I'm Samantha and this is Lucky and she's been crying all night. Not like her at all. I can't find anywhere that she's hurting though.'

The cat had been crying and he had to check it over? He looked at Kate and got a smug smile for his effort.

Right, you're on, girlfriend. I'm going to give this cat the best going-over it's ever had.

Crying could suggest something serious. Or a teenager who wanted attention via her pet. Then it struck him what he'd thought. Girlfriend? Kate? Not likely.

Swallowing hard, he turned to the girl. 'Come over to the table and I'll examine Lucky.'

'Sure. What's it like being a vet? I've always wanted to be one but Mum says it's not always nice when you have to do awful things to the animals.'

Again he glanced across to Kate and felt heat

in his face when she grinned at him as if she were saying 'told you so', which she hadn't, but still. She'd pay for that. In the nicest possible way, of course. He'd make sure she cooked dinner tonight, or bought in takeaways. 'Well, Samantha, your mother's right to a point, but there are many more times when it's the best job ever. Think of making a dog wag its tail again after having been hurt, or hearing a cat purr when you put her kittens on her belly.' He lifted Lucky out of the crate, and had to hold her tight when she tried to do a bunk. 'Hey, Lucky, no, you don't.'

Samantha reached for her pet and held her close while smoothing her fur. 'There you go, Lucky. This vet's going check you out to see why you cry so much.'

'Hold her on the table so I can feel all over her body.' He waited until Samantha had the cat on her haunches, still with a firm grip on it, before he began to carefully touch along her spine, then her ribs, and next her legs. 'All good so far.' Not a single reaction. 'Now I want to touch her stomach. She might not like that so be ready to hold her tighter.' Again no reaction. Finn straightened up. 'I think there's nothing wrong with Lucky. Maybe she's not crying but singing to you.'

Samantha stared at him. 'You think I don't know a cry when I hear it?'

Ouch. He needed to be more careful about

what he said. 'Sorry, I know you do, but Lucky didn't get distressed whenever I pressed her firmly and she would've if she had any serious injuries.'

Samantha suddenly smiled. 'Thanks, Doc. I mean, you are an animal doctor, aren't you? I'll take her home and bring my dog in for you to check out.' She swung Lucky up and into her basket. 'See you soon.' And away she went.

She was barely out of earshot when Kate and Mark started laughing.

'That went well, Doc,' Kate said through her laughter. 'This is starting to look like it might be a fun day.'

'Your turn next.' Finn grinned. 'I'll be right behind you, taking in every word you utter.'

'As long as it's not Samantha and her dog, though I suspect she'll want you to deal with that one.'

Di was laughing too. 'You forgot to try and sell her a toy for her cat.'

'Great. Now I've got to be a salesman as well.'

'And a dietician.' Kate pointed to the array of bagged dry pet food, then tapped other containers. 'These are bones, by the way.'

'I'm going to the coffee cart,' Mark interrupted them. 'Anyone want a hot drink?'

'I'll come with you,' Finn said when the order grew to five coffees of varying types. He'd have

gone if Mark was only getting one. He needed
to get away from the women giving him a hard
time about how he wouldn't know a plastic bone
from a real one.

'I can't believe how fast the day went,' Finn said
as he helped Kate unload the boot of her car at
the clinic after everyone had packed up the stall
once the crowd had finally dispersed. 'The hours
flew by.' It was now nearly five.

'That's because it was a lot of fun,' Kate answered as she hefted a carton half full of toys
out of her boot. 'We sold a lot of these.' The carton contained the remainder of what had been
in four boxes at the start of the day.

'Anyone would think it's Christmas the way
sales went.' He stretched his back and rolled his
shoulders before lifting the medical equipment
out of the boot and closing it. 'I'm looking forward to a drink on your deck when we get home
and watching the sun go down behind the mountains—if we're not too late.'

Bit of a mixed message there. Your deck and
then he'd said home as if it were his too. Despite
his concerns in a way it was, but becoming to
feel more and more like the go-to place when he
was ready to unwind after a hectic day—with
Kate, of course.

She dumped the carton in the storeroom and

headed outside again. 'See you there, then. First one home pours the drinks.'

'Or grabs the shower.' He stank after all the dogs, cats and guinea pigs he'd held and lifted and rubbed.

Kate laughed and leapt into her car. 'See you there.'

In the shower? Now there's a thought.

He'd love nothing more than to slip in behind her and lather that beautiful skin with soap. But first a challenge hung between them. 'You're on.'

Too late. She was halfway out of the entrance and heading for home.

Home. There it was again. Something he hadn't really had since his relationship with Amelia went south. He'd loved that feeling of belonging—to his home, to Amelia, to his life really. Except for Amelia, he missed it all. Even the bad days because they were as integral to life as the good ones. Since he'd moved into Kate's house there'd been more good than bad, but it had only been a week. They mightn't get along perfectly but they got along well enough for him to now be following her back there for a shower and a drink on the deck, ignoring his concerns.

He wasn't rushing, letting her get ahead, while he relaxed in the warmth exuding from his body. Perhaps he'd barbecue the chicken he'd bought at the supermarket yesterday, make a salad and bake some spuds to go with it all. Funny how his enjoyment for cooking had returned. Another small sign he was letting go the past and moving on as he'd hoped to.

When he parked up and went inside he could hear Kate singing to herself in her bedroom. 'You done with the bathroom?' he called.

Had he been that slow driving back? She usually had long showers. He'd often been tempted to join her under the water but sensed she might not appreciate that. So far he hadn't seen her fully naked. Somehow she always managed to remain partially covered with the duvet or clothes. Was that behind what she wouldn't talk about? If she *was* hiding anything. Whatever it was about, he didn't want to ask for fear of losing the closeness they had created together. See? She had got to him all too easily, which made him happy and wary all in one.

'Sure am. I feel so much better.'

The air was warm and moist in the hall outside her bedroom. The scent of roses teased him, heated parts of him that needed to remain cool. But couldn't. Kate did that so fast sometimes it was a wonder he could still walk.

The shower was on hot. Flicking it to cold, he got under the water and groaned as the chilly water poured all over him. Damn, it was freezing. Gritting his teeth, he withstood the chill until his skin was covered in goose bumps and the need tightening him lessened, then he flicked the tap back to hot, and got on with scrubbing himself hard all over in an attempt to keep Kate out of his mind. It worked to a point where he was finally clean and calm enough so that when he wandered out to the deck she didn't appear to notice anything out of the ordinary about him.

'Here, I got you a beer, but if you'd prefer a wine I can pour one.' She passed him a glass and a bottle, her smile beautiful, her eyes shining.

She was dressed in butt-hugging jeans that left nothing to his imagination, and a blouse that drew his eyes to the line between her breasts. 'Beer's good,' he said and took it from her. The bottle was cold, the beer chilly as it ran down his throat, but it did nothing to cool the parts of him that were overheating.

'It's been a fun day. Nothing like I'd expected,' Kate told him. 'I knew we'd be busy with people wanting us to see their animals, but I hadn't realised so many kids would be coming up to us wanting to show how great their pet was compared to everyone else's. It was sweet.'

'Even Samantha with her pets, and then her grandfather's dogs, was fun once she got over trying to impress us all.'

'A vet in the making, I wonder.' Kate was

standing right next to him and he could still smell roses.

'Were you like that as a teenager?'

'What? Chatting up the male vets in town?' She grinned. 'No way. I was too shy.'

'You? Shy? I don't believe it.' Somewhere along the way that had changed. There was nothing bashful about Kate. She did get hesitant at times when her past was mentioned but that was nothing to do with being shy. And today she'd been full-on happy and laughing with everyone and joining in all the races with pets, taking one or the other of her dogs with her. An ideal woman, if only he could trust her completely with his heart.

'Kate, sweetheart, you are beautiful.' Kate lay on her stomach, pressed up against Finn's gorgeous body, and breathed deep. Could Finn make love or what? That had been an amazing experience. The best lovemaking in for ever. There'd been no hesitation. He seemed to always want her for herself, not her beautiful face, but then he still hadn't seen what usually messed with her hope of love. Her fingers were spread across the scars. By not having to watch the horror appear in his eyes when they made love, she felt Finn had given her something so special she'd give him her heart if he would only open up to her more. Something she knew he wasn't doing, no matter how close they were getting.

'What are you smiling about?'

She blinked. So much for thinking he'd nodded off. 'That was amazing.'

'It was.' He leaned in and kissed her lightly. 'Is. I'm still feeling it.'

Laughter bubbled up her throat and spilled out between them. He really did make her feel so good. 'The perfect ending to a great day.'

'Who says that's the end of it?'

Her eyes widened. This was definitely different from anything she'd experienced in the past few years, even when she was still with Hamish. She shivered. This was not the time to be thinking about her ex. That was insulting to Finn, and her. Getting in a knot about her ex was spoiling this wonderful time with a man she was getting to care for more every day.

Rolling onto her side, she reached for him, and caressed him until he was tight and throbbing once more, making her hot and horny too.

Then Finn moved, and flipped her onto her back, touched her once and she was right there, ready and pulling him into her.

Finn woke to the sound of the shower door closing. A light sound that shouldn't have disturbed him so he must've been waking anyway. Reaching out to the other side of the bed, he felt the warmth where Kate had been lying. A picture of her under the spray of the shower had him up and striding to her bathroom in an instant. He was going to do this. It was another step in letting go of his fears. The urge to hold her against him, run his hands over that hot wet skin while he kissed the back of her slim neck, was huge. Damn, he was hardening again. Unbelievable.

Kate was standing under the shower, her face turned upward, her arms crossed under her breasts, her back to the door.

Sliding the glass doors apart, he stepped in behind her and slid his arms around her, tucked her in against him.

Kate instantly froze. 'Finn?'

'Who else?' What was going on here? Every muscle in her body felt tense. 'Kate, what's wrong?' He kept holding her. She hadn't pushed him away and he sensed she needed his strength, though why he had no idea. 'Kate, has someone hurt you in the past?'

Her shoulders rose, then dropped again.

He waited.

Slowly Kate turned in his arms, her face devoid of any emotion. But her eyes were fixed on him. She was waiting for something—from him.

Leaning in, he brushed a light kiss on her mouth before looking down her body to where her arms were tight against her upper abdomen. Below them scars crisscrossed all over her skin. Unreal. Her skin was a mess. But it was only skin. This was still Kate. Looking up, he gasped.

Her face was frozen, though pain was starting to emerge. She was terrified he'd make some obscene comment. He knew it, which meant someone else already had. 'Kate.' With one hand, he rubbed her back lightly. With the other he lifted her arms away, then touched her stomach as gently as possible. 'You are the most beautiful woman I've ever known.'

Her eyes widened but still she said nothing.

Leaning down, he kissed light trails all over her front, touching the scars, her breasts and neck.

He touched her breastbone. 'Beauty is on the inside too.'

'Too?'

'Absolutely. These scars are skin-deep, Kate. How you got them might've been horrendous. I don't know yet, but they don't make any difference to the wonderful woman I know.' Was this behind her mood swings? If so, surely she'd have realised he'd find out some time?

Tears coursed down her face, making his heart ache for her. 'I have changed since this happened. Men saw me as beautiful until I exposed myself in front of them.'

Hence why she kept the covers on the bed when they made love. 'When were you going to show me?' It did hurt that she hadn't done so at any point since they'd got together sexually. Not that she'd think about it when they were making out, but surely afterwards she would have?

'Did you think I'd treat you badly too?' Face it, trust was one of her issues and he understood that well, so he couldn't really get too upset about this.

Kate looked away, and drew a breath before locking her eyes on him again. 'I'm sorry. I kept putting it off because we were getting on so well and I didn't want that to stop.'

Fair enough. He understood too well, and could swallow his pride. 'Come here.' He wrapped his arms around her and held tight until the water started going cold. Reaching behind Kate, he turned it off and opened the shower, not letting her go. 'Come on. Let's get dry and tucked up in bed where it's warm.'

When she got out of the shower with him, he sighed in relief. She'd been so afraid of his reaction it made his blood boil. Obviously someone had been insulting about those scars. Someone? Or more than one man she'd tried to get close to? Who were they? Give him five minutes alone with them and they'd never do something so horrid again.

Picking up a towel from the rack, he began to rub her all over, drying her, showing her he didn't give a damn about the marks on her skin. Why would he? 'They're skin-deep, Kate, nothing more,' he repeated. He had to ignore how he felt about her not having told him from the start because he did want to move forward and trusting Kate had to be a part of that.

Nothing more than skin-deep.

Kate burst into tears again as she stared at this man drying her off. Not once had she seen his eyes widen in horror. There hadn't been a glimmer of shock. Finn accepted her as she was. Just like that. If she hadn't already begun falling for him, then she was certainly getting in deep now.

Then he wrapped her in her robe and swung her up in his arms to carry her back to bed. When they were both under the cover Finn pulled her close. 'How long ago did this happen, Kate? If you want to talk about it, that is.' He sounded cross, as if she'd let him down.

But then she had. She'd always been ready to explain if anyone asked, but so far no one had. Instead they'd thrown their hands up in horror, made awful comments and disappeared out of her life. Then along had come Finn and she'd wanted to hold onto him for as long as possible.

'It was when Hamish and I were in Northern

Queensland on that holiday I mentioned weeks ago. It was stinger season.' She knew her voice sounded flat, emotionless, but it was how she coped when telling the few people she had about what had happened.

Finn shuddered. 'I've heard those creatures can be nasty.'

'They are. All the beaches have stands where bottles of vinegar are placed so that if you get stung you can pour it on the area to relieve the pain.' Vinegar hadn't helped her that day. 'Hamish went in swimming despite the warning signs saying it was stinger season. Though he did wear a full wetsuit. He's an epileptic, and he had a fit while he was in the water. He'd gone quite a way out.'

She could see him now, splashing in the water, trying to wave to her and not succeeding. Fortunately she had seen what was happening. 'I saw him go under and thought that wasn't right somehow. When he came up again I recognised what was happening and raced in to haul him out, shouting for help as I went.'

Finn's arm tightened around her. 'You weren't wearing a wetsuit?'

'No. I had no intention of getting into the water at all, given it was stinger season. The surf lifesavers came out immediately. First they got Hamish out and while two dealt with him one came in for me. I was thrashing and screaming, trying to rush up onto the sand, but the pain from the stingers was unbearable. The guy dragged me onto his board and paddled like fury back to shore where someone poured vinegar all over me and others dried me and gave me water. Not a lot anyone could do, except wait to get me into an ambulance.'

She paused to let it sink in with Finn. She still couldn't believe he wasn't throwing his hands up in horror, and she well knew what to look for. 'I spent two nights in hospital and was told most people lose all trace of the scars over a period of time.'

'You were one of the unlucky ones.' He brushed a kiss on the top of her head. 'That must've been hard.'

'Not at first. I didn't get stung anywhere but my front between my bikini top and thighs. I mean, it's not as though my face was made to look awful. That would've been difficult because everyone would see and I know now their reactions would've been uncomfortable to say the least.'

'So what happened for you to change your mind?'

The hardest part of the whole episode.

'Hamish.'

Go on, get it over.

'At first he was sympathetic, and said he felt bad because if he hadn't had a fit then I wouldn't have gone into the water. It's not like he could help it. I'd do it again if I had to. It's what people do. Some people,' she added with a hint of bitterness. 'Sorry, but I still get upset.'

'You're allowed to. It's normal.' Finn brushed a kiss over her mouth, just like other times, no change. No withdrawal.

'Then three months later Hamish left me.' She could still see the look of despair on his face, as if he'd been doing his best by her and she'd failed him somehow. 'One night he was being snippy and when I asked what his problem was, he said he couldn't take it any more and that he was leaving. With that he got up off the sofa, went to his office by our bedroom to collect two cases of clothes he'd pre-packed and walked out the door.' She drew an unsteady breath and took another look at Finn to make sure she hadn't read him wrong, that he wasn't put off by any of her story.

He looked thoughtful, and when he noticed her watching him he asked, 'He left because of what happened in Queensland?'

'No. He'd only been staying on because it was his fault I went into the water and got so badly stung. Hearing that hurt as much as anything. The last thing I needed was for him to hang around out of guilt and nothing to do with loving me. That was over. His secretary was more alluring.' Kate couldn't help it. She smiled. 'She didn't stay around long. Got a new job and a new man.'

'No wonder you're smiling.' Finn smiled, then grew serious. 'Going back to when we met, I now understand why you looked like I'd stuck a knife in your chest that night I backed away from our kiss.' He sounded sad and apologetic all in one. 'I'm sorry, Kate. As I said at the time, that had nothing to do with you. It was me dealing with what Amelia had done and how I was nowhere near ready to get involved with another woman.'

Kate looked hard at this man who was making her the most comfortable she'd ever been with her body since that horrible day in Australia. 'I think I started to figure that out the night you told me what she'd done to you. You had no idea what I was hiding either.'

'Kate.' He paused. 'I get why you never let me see your body at first, but surely you must have known the time would come when I would see and want to know what had happened?'

'Yes, I did.' She sat back and clasped her hands together in her lap. This would go one of two ways. She could only hope Finn would continue to be understanding. 'The few times I was intimate with men I told them first, figured it would make things easier.'

'It didn't?'

'They both looked horrified but said things like it didn't make any difference. One of them I never saw again after the first night. The other guy hung around for a few days pretending he was coping but eventually he left too.'

'You didn't trust me enough to do the same? I did notice how you always kept covered when we weren't pressed so close together I couldn't have seen you anyway.'

Here we go. 'The first time we made love, it just happened. We were upset about putting down those horses and got together in a hurry. Raising the subject would've been a passion killer for sure.'

Finn was watching her with an unreadable face.

That hurt, but she couldn't really blame him. Digging deep, she continued. 'After that, I wanted to be with you so much I put it off. Being intimate with you has been so wonderful, and has made me happy about myself, and you. I should've told you. I know that. But I kept thinking one more time and then I'll tell him.'

'You have trust issues, too.'

Not the answer she was expecting, but then

this was Finn and she didn't do well when it came to reading him. 'I do. We do.'

'I can't promise not to hurt you, Kate, but, believe me, it won't be deliberate if I do.'

'I can live with that.' Not that she knew where they were going with their relationship yet.

'You do understand you're beautiful, don't you?' Finn slid a hand under her robe to lie on her abdomen, making her relax further. 'These are a part of life, a sign that you're kind and put others before yourself. Wear them with pride, Kate.'

She stared at him. 'You are amazing.' He had no idea what he'd done for her. 'Thank you so much.'

'For what? Being honest? That's easy.' He wrapped her in a hug and held tight.

Kate could not believe this. All she'd ever wanted from a man was to be accepted for all parts of her and here Finn was showing it was possible. She burst into tears. Doing that a lot tonight.

He rubbed her back as she sobbed. Another good point for Finn. Hamish had always disappeared in a hurry whenever she'd cried, which meant she'd learned not to most of the time.

Slowly she quietened. 'Thank you, Finn. You have no idea how good you've made me feel.' Almost back to the woman she used to be, though she'd never be quite the same. Life's lessons had a lot to say. Now she could see that she'd always overreacted after Hamish had left her. He was supposed to have loved her for ever, and instead had made her uncomfortable about the scars because if he couldn't handle them, then who could?

'Stop it, Kate. I get that it's been a difficult time for you, but from now on don't let the past get in the way of what you want in the future. You can have it all if you don't let other people destroy your dreams.'

'I am finally starting to see that. You've upped the ante for me.'

Blimey, Finn certainly knew his way into a woman's heart. He was wonderful. But caution still held her from leaping into his arms and never letting go. He had said he had trust issues and so far she didn't know how deep those went after all the time since his relationship with Amelia had gone so hideously wrong. Amelia had done a number on him that would take some coming back from. It wouldn't be easy to let another woman into his heart or anywhere near his possessions.

Only time would show Finn that he could trust a woman he might care about. She wanted to be that woman, and because of that would hold back from throwing herself at him. Hopefully, living here, he might get to see she was worthy of his trust, because she didn't have it in her to do to Finn, or anyone, what Amelia had done. 'Maybe you should heed your own advice,' she told him gently.

'Valid point. I'll see what I can do. Now shall we move on and enjoy the rest of the evening?' Without waiting for her answer, Finn rose from the bed and found his shirt and shorts. 'Stay there. I have an idea on how to finish this evening.'

A few minutes later he returned with a glass of wine each. 'Dinner in bed.'

It was easy to laugh. She felt so good. It was as though a boulder had been lifted away, and she could breathe freely for the first time in more than two years. 'Cheers.' She tapped his glass with hers, still unable to fully accept he hadn't hurt her when he saw the scars.

Finn took the tray back to Kate's bedroom and set it on her bedside table. 'Toasted sandwiches with ham, cheese and red onion.' Easy to make and easier to eat in bed than steak and salad.

'Great.' Kate was smiling softly, as though her life had changed for the better this evening.

All because of his reaction. He had no doubt about that. She'd been expecting the worst and he hadn't delivered. There was no need. He didn't see the scarring as a problem. 'Can't say I've ever had a dinner date in bed before.' He was still reeling at what her ex had done to her though. Or, for that matter, the other men. How could anyone be critical of her scars? They weren't pretty but they did not mean there was something wrong with Kate. She was beautiful inside and out, and marks on her skin were never going to alter that.

'If this is a date, then I'd like more of them.'

He watched her face begin to colour up and, before she got too flustered, said, 'I'll have to see what else I can come up with.'

Was their fling about to become more meaningful? Was he ready? Not when he still had so many trust issues of his own to deal with. It had hurt to hear Kate say she'd put off telling him about the scars. That suggested she didn't fully trust him. She was right not to. He hadn't, and still wouldn't, mention how Amelia had fooled him into believing she was pregnant. That would mean going further than he was prepared to do.

On the other hand, Kate was wonderful, and he wanted more of her. To him Kate's bombshell had been a fizzer. It didn't matter that Kate wasn't physically perfect. Perfection was a little too OTT at times.

So, the big question for him. Did he want to be in a relationship with Kate? Did he only want more sex without serious commitment? Or did he want the whole show? He knew what he wanted. He just didn't believe he was ready. Despite the delay in revealing her biggest fear, Kate was honest, and he knew she was trustworthy. But deep inside he still didn't accept he could let go and totally trust anyone with his heart. Not yet. Not even Kate. Because he was beginning to fall for her, she had the power to hurt him so much and that was something he could not face again.

Yet he did so want to have more with her. What if he lost any chance with her by not leaping in and going for the lot? Better to be careful, than be hurt. Or was it? He had no answer to that at the moment. Kate was also vulnerable. She'd been hurt by her husband and he couldn't be responsible for that happening again either. So did he continue looking for somewhere else to live or stay here and see how everything played out?

Kate nudged him. 'If you're trying to think up other crazy dates, then stop. It's sidetracking you and I'd prefer to enjoy your company now while we eat these scrumptious sandwiches with our wine.'

'Fair cop.' Focus on the moment, and stop questioning everything. He bit into a sandwich and agreed it was delicious, even if he'd made it.

'This was not how I expected the day to end.' Kate was smiling to herself.

'What were you expecting?'

She shrugged. 'Hadn't a clue really, but hot sex with a dinner-in-bed date was not it.'

'The unexpected is often the best.' Especially when it included sex with a stunning woman. He looked at the empty plate. 'Do you want me to make some more sandwiches?' He had made what he thought was a lot.

'Not for me. I've pigged out enough.'

'I'll put the dogs on dishes duty.'

'They'd love you.'

That was love he wasn't afraid of. Moving closer to Kate, he finished his last sandwich and went with feeling happy. It was kind of special sitting in bed with her, having a wine and eating dinner. Yes, he could get to more than like doing things like this on a regular basis.

'You know I'm not going back to my room tonight, don't you?' He couldn't leave her tonight when she'd bared her fears to him. She might get the wrong idea and think he'd been put off by what he'd seen despite saying otherwise.

'I'd tie you to the headboard if I thought there was a chance of that happening.'

'Sounds kinky.' He chuckled.

CHAPTER NINE

THE DAYS FLEW BY. Having Finn in her life made everything seem wonderful. The sky was bluer, the sun warmer. Her heart felt lighter. Kate stretched out in the bed three weeks later, smiling from ear to ear. She and Finn were getting along so well she had to keep pinching herself to believe it was real. She had a store of memories involving hot, sensual sex most nights to prove it was all true, but there were also the nights they didn't share the sheets because one or other of them was exhausted after a busy day at work. On those nights she'd love to curl up with Finn and fall asleep in his arms, but it wasn't to be.

That was when she missed Finn the most even though he was only across the hallway. Apart from the night he'd seen her scars he always went back to his bed after they made love and so it made sense that when they didn't he didn't come to her bed at all.

She couldn't help feeling superfluous to requirements when he didn't want to make love.

It wasn't because her body made him cringe because he'd done it before then. She suspected he wasn't ready for more than they already had going, and worried that he was seeing this as a fling with no real future. That he might never want more from her. It was hard to take as she was falling for him more and more by the day and therefore putting her heart on the line. Better to try to win him over and lose, than back off completely without knowing what he felt. Or so she kept telling herself when the doubts flared.

Woof. Woof.

In other words, *Where's our food? And why aren't we out walking already?*

Sam and Rusty were at the door.

'Coming, guys.' No rest for the wicked, or the busy vet.

Dressed and out in the kitchen, she filled her pets' bowls and made a plunger of coffee to give her a kick-start to the day.

Finn had left a note on the bench.

Hey, there. Gone to visit a goat farmer who has animals with mastitis. See you later. X

She smiled and blew a kiss in the air. He made her heart sing. It seemed strange having the house to herself. Most mornings she and Finn bumped around each other in the kitchen and bathroom as they got ready for work, laughing and chatting as though they'd always done that.

At the end of the day they usually shared dinner, though he visited his parents one night a week and some nights went to see his brother. She'd been a bit disappointed when she hadn't been asked to go along even once because it kind of said they weren't in a serious relationship. Finn usually made up for it when he got home and joined her in bed for a busy hour, wiping out any concerns she had about where they were at.

He hadn't talked any more about his past. It seemed he'd told her all he was willing to, and she had to accept that, like it or not. She was happy to have got her problems out of the way and was starting to be herself in all respects. The old Kate had no hang-ups about herself and was willing to share all she had. Finn's ready acceptance of her had opened her heart to possibilities for her future, even *their* future.

Picking up the leads, she muttered to her boys, 'Let's go somewhere different today.' She'd do something out of routine, all because she felt happy. She'd drive to Kirwee and walk around the park and the showgrounds so they could run free for a while. Nothing like a good walk to get the day under way. Along with coffee, which she needed to feel fully awake. Lately she had been feeling more tired than usual, which had to be because of all the activity she and Finn got up to.

After filling her coffee holder, she headed out

to the car with the dogs bouncing along beside her. Life was good, when she wasn't worrying about what Finn thought of their relationship that didn't appear to really be a relationship. Not one where they were getting serious about each other anyway. Friends with benefits still best described what was going on, which dampened her spirits because she did want more.

Her heart was getting involved deeper and deeper by the day, but she doubted Finn's was. He might have lightened up with her, but he still held a lot back. It was there in the way he didn't share more than his body, meals and work. Maybe that was enough for now, and she was rushing things, but she'd waited a long time for a man like Finn to come into her life and it was nigh on impossible to go slow. He was everything she wanted. And some.

'Feel like a meal at the pub?' Kate asked Finn on Friday after the clinic closed. 'I can't be bothered cooking and I am not expecting you to do it either.'

'Good, because I had no intention of doing anything more exciting than ordering in takeaways.' He was ready to sit down with a beer and unwind from a busy week dealing with too many goats with mastitis and sheep with blowfly strike. The second one had had him showering so often his skin had become very dry. Going to the pub with Kate was a perfect end to a busy day. She'd soon make him laugh and forget work.

'Whichever we go for, it's my shout.' Kate had changed out of her scrubs and dressed in those jeans that highlighted her cute butt and flat stomach while doing indescribable mischief to his libido.

It wasn't hard for her to grab his attention. He was smitten with her. She gave so much of herself even though there were still moments when she held back, as if more than the scarring was an issue. Either that or she only wanted some fun and nothing more.

It had been a busy week at night-time, which had nothing to do with animals. And that, plus not knowing what Kate thought, made the decision he'd been mulling over since a phone call he'd received from a rental company earlier in the day difficult. Suddenly there were two houses available and he had to make up his mind fast about which one to take as there were other people also desperate for rental accommodation. Peter was a mate of the agent, hence him getting first dibs.

Finn's problem was that he also had to decide whether to carry on living in Kate's house or move out. He knew he'd miss sharing the evening meals and other everyday things if he went, which worried him, though not as much as it once would've.

They were great together. Everything was going well. Almost too well. As it had done last time he'd got into a serious relationship. Though he doubted Kate saw it as serious at this point. She still held back on her feelings just enough to have him wondering what she thought about them together. Something he also avoided thinking too much about.

Except the time had come to decide what he really wanted going forward. Stay on with Kate and see how it worked out, or set himself up in another property and take time to get closer to her? If that was possible with his fear of being hurt again still hovering in the background, though not as strong as it used to be.

'Hello, Finn? Are you with me or not?' Kate sounded peeved.

'Making a call on what to do about dinner,' he said. 'Let's go to the pub for a drink first and decide what to do about eating after that.' There'd be a crowd there so serious conversation would be difficult with all the noise going on around them, which might give him time to think more about the rental properties and what he was going to do. He was coming to enjoy living in the community, which added to the ease of settling down. Not as much as he loved being with Kate, by a long way, but he could admit to wanting to settle down and this was a step in the right direction.

'We have a plan. See you there.'

'Let's walk. The parking's always diabolical there.' Not waiting for an answer, Finn took Kate's hand and led them outside, locking the door behind him. 'Any plans for the weekend?'

'Mow Dad and Mum's lawns since they'll be home next week. Mine need a cut too. Otherwise not a lot.' She glanced at him as if he might have a plan for them to do something together.

He wasn't taking her to see the houses. Not when he was in two minds about whether to ask her if he could stay on with her or go it alone while he got himself more set up for the future. This was something he had to decide for himself, by himself. Kate was important to him, but he wasn't letting her that close. Not yet.

'I have a couple of chores to do in the morning, then I want to check on the goats I've been treating all week.'

'Sounds exciting.' She smiled sadly.

'The thing is, it is in a way. I like getting out on a farm amongst the animals. It reminds me why I became a vet in the first place.'

'And why was that?'

Surely he'd mentioned it before? 'I love the outdoors and animals so it's a given really. I once thought of doing medicine—as in for humans—but figured I could have my cake and eat it too if I became a vet. Then I went and set up a city practice instead, which made no sense at all.'

But he had been in love with Amelia and doing what he'd believed was the right thing by supporting her and moving to her home town. This time he'd do it differently. He was working rurally, and planned to have a specialist practice on the side later on. No rush for anything. One step at a time. Like with Kate. If there was going to be a next time with her, as in a relationship involving everything from love to trust to having a family, he had to get it right for both hearts involved. 'Not everything goes according to plan, does it?'

Her laugh was tight. 'Can't argue with that. I suppose it would be too boring if everything ran true to schedule. Though there are things I wish hadn't gone haywire for me, I'm still happy with most aspects of my life.'

'I'm glad to hear it.' Had she moved on from her scarring all because he'd seen it and hadn't made a big deal out of it? Or had she already been inching closer to that all on her own and he'd helped her by being honest? She deserved better than how her ex had treated her. But who didn't?

Stepping inside the pub, he paused. 'Unbelievable. It's only half full and nowhere near as noisy as usual.'

'Make the most of it,' Kate answered. 'You still want a beer?'

'Please.' He named the brand he preferred. 'I'll be over at that table in the corner.' As he watched Kate make her way through the tables to the bar, his heart was heavy. So he *was* going to move out of her place. He had to. Despite caring so much for Kate, he was not ready to give his heart away completely. He hadn't seen the houses yet, but he liked the sound of the small one-bedroom cottage on a twenty-acre block owned by a couple who lived on the property too. The agent had arranged for him to see it at ten in the morning plus meet the owners. The other house was further away and larger, so, for him, less appealing.

'Here you go.' A glass of beer appeared in front of him.

'That was quick.'

'Helps to know the bar lady. Or her cat anyway.' Kate sat her derrière on a stool and lifted her glass to her lips, bringing heat to his skin thinking about them trailing kisses all over his body.

'You seem to have a lot on your mind tonight.' She cut through his quandary. 'Want to share? Halve the load?'

'Not really. Thanks all the same, but I'd prefer to sit back and unwind after the crazy week. Were you busy in the clinic today?'

Kate stared at him for a full minute, disappointment darkening her eyes, before she shook her head and sipped her G and T. Finally she answered quietly, 'No more than usual.'

He'd blown the relaxed atmosphere he craved between them. But telling her what was going on in his head would've done that too. Even more so. Except the time was fast approaching when he had to tell her what he was doing. He'd wait until he'd chosen which property to rent. Of course he was putting it off. He didn't want to see more disappointment in those beautiful eyes. And he wanted just a little more quiet time with her. He cared for Kate. More than cared, and was on the way to falling in love with her, so he did not want to hurt her in any way.

'Think I'll head home after this.' Kate held her glass between them. 'I don't feel like fish and chips tonight.'

In other words, she'd changed her mind about spending time with him. Fair enough. He was letting her down.

Kate closed her father's garden shed with a bang and headed for her car. She'd hit the local supermarket to grab some groceries before going home to mow her own lawns. The headache she'd earlier swallowed paracetamol to kill was still throbbing behind her eyes. A sleepless night tossing and turning for hour after hour had done its number on her, especially as she'd been exhausted already.

Something was up with Finn and she knew she wasn't going to like whatever it was. He'd been in a right old mood at the pub last night. Definitely hiding something, which got her back up. For months Hamish had hidden the fact he'd fallen out of love with her and when she had learned what was going on she'd been equally hurt that he didn't love her and that he hadn't had the guts to tell her, blaming the stinger incident for his reticence.

Apparently she and Finn weren't a couple, weren't in love, but they had shared a lot lately, so why the hell couldn't he be straight with her? Her blood was fizzing as she thought about his attitude last night and how he'd shut her down enough for her to know he was not being open with her. That really annoyed her. Even if they were only friends with benefits, she deserved better.

But—and it was a huge but—she had to tell him her news. No holding back as she had about her scars. This had to be done, and sooner rather than later.

When Kate pulled up in her driveway beside Finn's ute she didn't know whether to be pleased he was home or worried about the outcome of what she had to tell him. Lugging the grocery bags inside, she called out, 'Hi there. How's your morning been?'

No reply. Was he outside somewhere?

She began putting the groceries away, and felt her skin tighten. Turning around, she saw Finn leaning against the door frame. 'Hello. You look worried. What's happened?'

For a long moment he said nothing.

Her heart began thumping, and the headache intensified. 'Finn?'

'Kate, I've found a house to rent and as it's available immediately I'm moving out today.'

She grabbed the edge of the bench to hold herself upright. Hadn't seen that coming, had she? Yet it did explain why he'd been short with her last night. 'You never said a word, even when I asked what you had planned for this morning.'

'No, I didn't. I have been in two minds about whether to rent or carry on living here.'

'The house won, I see.' She knew she sounded angry but, hell, she was sad more than anything and that was an emotion he wasn't going to know about.

'I had two to look at, and the one I'm going to is just along the road in Kirwee. It's a one-bedroom cottage overlooking paddocks. Ideal, really.'

Ideal? Living with her wasn't so great after all. 'Here I was thinking we were getting along very well and that we had something going between us.' She was losing her cool. Blame it on the headache and the pain in her heart. Blame it on the news she had yet to tell him. Hell, blame it on anything. It didn't matter. Finn was leaving—today.

He moved into the room and sat on a stool. 'Kate, I am so sorry. We *are* getting on well, and that doesn't have to stop. The thing is I'm not ready to be in a full-on relationship. I need my own space.'

Leaning against the counter, she stared at him. 'That's honest, I suppose. Well, here's some news for you. I am just over four weeks pregnant.'

The stool hit the floor as he leapt to his feet. 'Oh, no, you don't. I am not going down that path again.' He about turned and charged to the door where he stopped and turned to stare at her, despair all over his face.

'Finn?' she said as calmly as it was possible to be, which wasn't easy when her heart was breaking out of her chest. 'Talk to me.'

'I believed in you, Kate.'

'Why change your mind?' She was pregnant,

not about to slice his heart out of his chest. Or had she just done that?

Finn continued to stare at her as though she were a monster.

She gaped at him. What was going on? It was a shock, she'd accept that. She was still coming to grips with the fact she was carrying a baby, but Finn's reaction was way over the top. 'I can show you the test result if that would make it easier for you to accept.'

His mouth dropped open as disbelief filled his face. 'No, thanks. I am not such a sucker as to run with that.' He turned away, stepped through the door.

Kate's head spun while her chest pounded with pain. She had no idea what this was about. 'Finn, stop,' she begged. 'Why are you being so hurtful?'

He turned back. 'You expect me to believe you?' Sarcasm dripped off his tongue, so thick Kate sagged.

She wasn't getting anywhere. 'You don't believe me? Or you don't want to?'

'Both,' he snapped.

The air left her lungs in a rush. Never had she thought he could be so harsh, so rigid in his reaction to her news. This was a new Finn, not the man she'd come to love. 'You owe me an explanation. I didn't get pregnant by myself.'

'Really?'

A baby was a huge issue to take on board. She got that in loads since learning about her pregnancy yesterday. She was still getting her head around it, but Finn was way out of line here. They were in this together, whether he liked it or not.

'Thanks a lot. For the record, I would never lie to you. I might've taken my time about the scars, but I did not lie to you.' She turned away, unable to look any longer at the man who'd got under her radar and stolen her heart. She'd always known this day would come, but hadn't expected it to be because she was pregnant with his child. And certainly not so hurtful she felt as though her body were falling apart. 'I deserve better than this,' she muttered.

Silence engulfed the room.

She hadn't heard Finn leave so presumed he was still standing in the doorway. Well, he could stand there all he liked. She wasn't going to relent and make it easy for him.

When she could no longer stand the silence she gave up trying to be tough and turned to face him. 'Please go, Finn. Now.' He had somewhere to sleep tonight, and even if he hadn't she would still kick him out.

'I'm on my way, but…' He paused and swallowed hard as though getting himself under control. 'I'm sorry it's come to this.'

'Really?'

'And here I was thinking we were getting on brilliantly, no pressure on each other, accepting we both have issues with our pasts. Idiot.'

Finn was still watching her as though he didn't know what to do next.

'Go. Now.'

Get the hell out of here before I burst into tears or throw something at you.

Thankfully he did.

She spun around and picked up the loaf of bread she'd brought home with the groceries to bang down on the pantry shelf, followed by a box of teabags, a packet of coffee beans, a tin of peaches, eggs, sugar, rice.

'Damn you, Finn Anderson,' she shouted. 'Damn you for that first kiss, and all the sex that followed, and for being so damned kind and understanding.'

Except he hadn't been that understanding when she'd said she was pregnant. Not at all. She dropped to her knees, her head in her hands, and gave into the tears pouring all over her face. Now she really understood and felt the truth of what she'd done. 'Damn you for stealing my heart.'

CHAPTER TEN

FRIDAY MORNING AND the clinic was flat-out busy. It had been that way since the school pet fair.

Kate wasn't buzzing, hadn't felt at all happy since Finn had walked out on her news. She did try, unsuccessfully, to join in the enthusiastic talk about the success of the day as she swallowed lukewarm coffee. 'I think we've gained quite a few more patients.'

'Like we need to be any busier,' quipped Mark. Then he looked at Peter. 'Sorry, boss. Didn't mean it.'

Peter grunted. 'You have a point though. I am going to advertise for another vet, preferably someone keen on the rural side of things. Gavin's coming back full-time next week but he doesn't want to work with cattle.'

'Can't say I blame him,' Kate muttered, glancing at Finn, who appeared more interested in his coffee than what was going on around him. If only she were able to go over and hug him tight to help remove that sad expression he'd been wearing for days, but nothing was ever as simple as that. Besides, he'd probably leap up and walk out of the room, leaving her with a load of questions she had no answers for.

'Finn, know anyone who might like to join you out in the paddocks?'

Finn finally looked up. 'No one comes to mind, but I'll give it some thought over the day and get back to you.'

'Good.' Peter stood up. 'Guess we're done here so let's get the day under way. Have a good one everybody.'

'If only,' Kate thought as she gathered her notepad and pen, and stood up to go to the treatment room. The only good thing about today was that it was Friday and the weekend lay ahead. Hopefully she'd manage a little more sleep. She'd barely slept a wink since Finn left two weeks ago, and now just one look at him and her heart broke all over again.

He might've thrown her under the bus but she missed him so much. Nothing felt right any more. As if she were treading water while trying to keep up with herself. It was as if she'd been living a lie with Finn yet she still didn't really believe that. He was too tender and caring to be the angry man who'd snapped when she'd told him she was pregnant. She'd spent hours wondering what that was about and had come up with nothing other than maybe it was something Amelia had done that had hurt him badly.

'What's up first?' she asked Di, who was walking beside her.

'I think it's Percy, the rabbit. He's got a swollen foot this time.'

Percy was known to suffer any number of ailments because his owner, a little old lady with nothing else to do but spend all her time with her pet, kept imagining problems.

'A saline solution should see to that.' Kate smiled grimly. If only everything were so easily fixed, but saline solution would do nothing for her heart.

'I think Finn's going out to see Doria's other horses this morning. That will be hard after having to put the other two down after that accident.'

Why tell her that? She didn't need to know what Finn had on his plate for the day.

'It will be.'

The accident that had led to the second kiss she and Finn had shared. Followed by sensational sex. She didn't call it lovemaking any more. She might've been falling for Finn, but obviously that hadn't been the same for him. Pain hit her. She missed him like she'd never have believed. She'd known she was falling for him, but had had no idea just how deep she'd got. She loved him. That was it in black and white.

'Hey, Di, you got a minute?' Finn called from the other end of the hallway, sending a shiver down Kate's back. 'I need some info on Doria's horses that you've got somewhere.'

Di turned back. 'Sure. It's all in the system but I've also got a file in my desk I can lend you.'

Kate pretended not to notice the way her heart rate increased at the sound of that sexy voice. If this was how she reacted now, then the days and weeks ahead were going to be downright difficult to get through.

But, and her back straightened, she was not going anywhere. This was the job she loved. The people she liked working with were here, and she could get through anything that came her way, even seeing Finn often. They were back to being colleagues, not friendly workmates. She was broken hearted, but she was alive and kicking. She would cope, no matter what. She had to.

Finn had helped her get past the scarring problem and she would not go back to being fearful of what a man might think of her scars. Thanks to Finn, that was over. He had rejected her for reasons unknown but this time she wasn't letting that take over her life. She was still looking ahead, not over her shoulder.

* * *

Finn watched Kate slowly walk into the treatment room. She looked as tired as he felt, if not more so. Was she not sleeping either? Or was the pregnancy affecting her already? He didn't know if it was too early for her to start feeling out of sorts yet. Anyway, he was probably looking for an excuse so that he didn't have to face the truth—he'd let Kate down badly. In fact, he'd hurt her terribly.

The instinct to protect his heart had made him walk away without explaining his reaction, a terrible thing to have done when he'd expected honesty from her all the time. She'd trusted him with her truth. He should've done the same.

It isn't too late.

Or it might be. Only one way to find out. First he owed her an apology. A big one. A genuine one. One that let her know he'd be there for their baby no matter what happened between them. Kate deserved the best from him. So did their child.

'Where're you off to first?' Peter was back.

'Got to see Doria's other horses.'

'Can you go out to Johnson's after that? One of the milking goats has mastitis.'

'No problem.' He dumped his mug in the sink and headed away, trying to leave Kate behind, but she followed him with images in his head of her naked body under his, dishing up their dinner, laughing and talking together. Of the shock and pain when he'd refused to hear her out when she'd said she was pregnant.

How could he let her go? Face it. He couldn't. Everything he wanted was right here if he had the guts to go for it. Had the courage to move on and give his heart to her. Would she give him a second chance? He needed to take the risk anyway, beg her to forgive him if he had to. Deep down he knew she wouldn't hurt him. Not deliberately. But she might walk away. Sometimes a person had to take risks. If *he* didn't then he was never going to get over what Amelia did and therefore he wouldn't have a wonderful life with a fabulous woman and that baby growing inside her. Their baby.

So what was he going to do about it? he wondered for the umpteenth time. Kate wouldn't let him back in as easily as he'd wished for. He couldn't blame her. He'd been so quick to react against her news that he'd have a hard time convincing her he'd not do something like that again.

As he pulled into the farmyard where Doria waited for him, he heaved a sigh. At least he had the day to think about everything and hopefully come up with the right answers to all the questions flipping through his head.

* * *

'Hello, Kate.' Finn stood on her deck, looking tense and worried.

Which upped the anxiety tightening her as she walked across the yard towards him, determined not to let him get to her. Not until she knew why he was here anyway, and then only if it was about something that would make her happy.

Her heart sank lower than it already was. Whatever had brought Finn here, she doubted it would be anything to get excited about. He'd been so blunt when she'd told him about the baby that there was no way he could've put that behind him and want to move forward with her.

Unfortunately, now he was here it was hard not to rush over and throw herself into his arms and never let go. Seeing him at work every day had only intensified the pain of not being able to relax with him over a meal or drink, and made her more determined that she wasn't going to be made a fool of again.

'Hello, Finn. I didn't expect to see you this weekend.'

'I'm sure you didn't.'

'What's this about?'

'I'd like to talk about us, and the baby.'

So he wasn't about to get down on bended knee and say he loved her. No surprise there.

Stepping around him, she said, 'Come inside. It's chilly out here now that autumn's making its presence felt.'

He followed her in without a word, which worried her further. He wasn't a big talker, but she'd have thought he'd want to get whatever he'd come to say off his chest so he could leave again.

Closing the door, she went into the lounge and sat on the sofa.

Finn took the chair opposite.

Looking directly at the man she was trying hard not to show how much she loved, she asked, 'What's up?'

'Kate, I am so sorry for not immediately believing you about the baby.' He stood up and paced to the window and back, sat down again. 'But I do believe you. I did almost immediately after my outburst. It was obvious you were telling the truth by the way you spoke and the stunned look in your eyes when I reacted how I did. I couldn't be more sorry if I tried.'

Once again he'd stunned her. 'I'm six weeks along.' Her eyes were locked on him, as though daring him to trust her. She still didn't think he fully believed her.

'Kate, I truly accept we're having a baby.'

She wasn't rolling over. 'Why didn't you come and talk to me earlier, then?'

'Because I didn't realise that I was stuck in the

past and therefore ignoring the fact I was well on the way to finding the future I so dearly want. You've done that for me, Kate.'

She tried to relax, but there was more to come. At the very least, she needed to know what role he thought he'd have in their child's life. 'That's a start, I suppose.' She wasn't being very forgiving, but she had a broken heart to protect. And a baby that needed her.

Finn stood in the middle of the room, watching her. How the hell had he managed to walk away? She was everything he wanted. He loved everything about her. 'Kate, I need to tell you what else happened between Amelia and me.'

'Go on.'

She wasn't making this easy, but then he could hardly blame her after the way he'd reacted about the pregnancy. Deep breath. 'After I found out about the bankruptcy and then Amelia's gambling addiction, I was gutted. Angry. And hurt. I spent a lot of time trying to figure out where to go from there. Amelia had done a number on me and I struggled with that. But I also understood that addiction is not something that goes away because a person wants it to.'

Kate remained quiet. Was that good or bad?

He continued. 'I went to stay with a friend while I got my head around everything. Amelia went home to her parents, who thought I was the guilty party because I should've seen what was going on. They might've had a point. Who knows?'

Again she said nothing, making his heart thump heavily.

'Two weeks after everything blew up in our faces, Amelia came to tell me she was pregnant and suggested we try again.' He stopped. Inhaled again and continued laying his heart out there for Kate to see all the cracks. 'I wasn't going to walk away from my child so I knew I had to work something out. We agreed I'd move in with her at her family's home until I got a job and could pay for a rental property. I got a job within days at a local vet clinic.'

He looked away, staring out of the window for a long moment. This was it. The real crux to everything that had gone down with Kate. 'At the end of my first week some of the staff invited me to the pub as a welcome gesture. I couldn't say no, even though it meant forking out money for a round of drinks I didn't have spare.'

Kate nodded in understanding. 'Fair enough.' She wasn't giving anything away.

Finn watched her, his head and heart filled with sorrow. He wasn't getting anywhere with this. Might as well get it over and done and leave. 'I walked into the pub and there was Amelia, dressed to the nines in clothes I'd never seen before, drinking and chatting up a man at the bar. Drinking while pregnant? That made my blood boil. I went up to her and demanded she come outside to talk to me. Surprisingly, she did, and that's when I learned she was not pregnant, and never had been. It had been a ruse to get me on side so she didn't have to go without anything until she found another, richer man. Which she did within a very short time.'

Kate locked a fierce gaze on him. 'You outright rejected me at the mention of the pregnancy. No matter what happened in the past, I did not deserve that. It's no excuse for accusing me of not telling the truth.'

He deserved that, but it still hurt. 'I'm not making an excuse. I'm explaining. I don't want your sympathy. You deserve the truth. I didn't think I was ready to give my heart away again. But over these past two weeks I've missed you so much I feel I'm continuously breaking into little pieces.'

She sat, her back straight as possible and her head high. 'You think I'd do anything half as bad to you as Amelia did?'

'No, Kate, I don't. Not at all.' Never.

Her face softened.

Was that a good sign? Was this going to work out after all? He waited patiently.

'You've helped me through the rough stuff, too. I feel whole again.'

Wow. Finn risked reaching for her hands, and sighed with relief when she didn't withdraw them. 'You're amazing. You know that?'

Kate blinked. How could she stay mad at Finn? He'd laid everything out for her to see and know what drove him. A small laugh escaped. It felt so good to have her hands held in his. This was Finn, the man she'd inadvertently given her heart to. She didn't want it back. But they weren't out of the woods yet.

'I wasn't up front with you about my problems, Finn, and I regret that. But it also helps me understand why you lashed out when I told you I was pregnant. I can't believe Amelia lied to you about being pregnant.' Talk about a manipulative woman.

'Which is why whenever I came up with a reason to stay with you, I found another to go. I was fighting putting everything behind me because it seemed too risky when really all I had to do was look forward.' His hands tightened around hers. 'Kate, sweetheart, from now on I'm all about getting on with living the life I've always dreamed about. I love you so much, Kate. I really do.'

Wow. Finn loved her. All the tightness around

her heart melted in a flash. Dreams really did come true. There was a flutter in her stomach, and a lightness in her head.

Take this slowly, Kate.

True. She was so relieved about what he'd told her that instead of taking it slowly and working through it all she was rushing in without stopping to consider everything. So she slowed everything down by asking, 'How do I know you won't reject me again?'

His eyes widened and he stared at her for a long moment. 'Is that how you see it? No, don't answer that because that's exactly what I did.' His chest rose and fell rapidly. 'It was instinctive to protect myself. I didn't stop to absorb what you said. If I had I wouldn't have said those things. I swear I wasn't rejecting you deliberately, Kate.' His face was full of remorse.

Her heart turned over. She knew what it was like to have her heart broken, so understood where he was coming from. She hadn't always dealt with her hurt very well either. 'Can you see us working through future problems together?'

'I don't want it any other way. But I can't promise that I won't make mistakes as we go along either.'

'Nor can I. We're normal, I guess.' Did she hold out any longer? He'd not held back in answering her questions. Anyway, what was the point when she knew exactly what she wanted? That was to open her heart to him completely, to be honest and open.

'Finn, I love you. I have done for a while.' The pain of watching him leave the other week had finally been replaced by love and warmth and relief, no more hesitation. 'Damn it, Finn, I love you so much it hurts. In a nice way.'

He was up on his feet and hauling her into his arms, his mouth coming closer and closer until he covered hers with those sensual lips she'd missed. She fell in against him, her hands feeling his warmth as she ran them up and down his back. He kissed her deeply, a kiss filled with promise and love and a future.

Tipping her head back, she stared at the man who'd changed her life for ever in the best way possible. 'Finn,' she whispered, and swallowed. Started over. 'Finn, we've both had trust issues so we understand each other well. I am totally in love with you. I can't imagine living my for ever without you.'

'Back at you.' He drew a deep breath. 'And our child.'

'And our child.' She nodded, her smile getting wider and wider. Then those wonderful lips returned to hers, pressing hard, devouring her with a kiss that was better than any she'd ever experienced with him. That said it all. She loved Finn. He loved her.

He said softly, 'Sweetheart, I can't believe this.'

She tipped her head back and smiled like crazy. 'I can.'

'I'll be pinching myself so often just to remind myself how lucky I am that I'll be black and blue all over. You're the best thing ever to happen to me.' Finn swung her up into his arms and headed for her bedroom. From now on their bedroom.

She'd found the man of her dreams, and she wasn't letting him go.

Monday morning and the usual meeting before the week got properly under way. Kate sat beside Finn in the tearoom, trying hard not to look besotted, and knowing she was failing. There'd been a permanent grin on her face since Finn had told her he loved her. In between packing up Finn's few belongings and shifting them back to her house, where this time his clothes were sharing her wardrobe, they'd spent a lot of the weekend showing just how much they loved each other. Her bed had never had such a workout. Or her body.

'Right, I think that's everything,' Peter said. 'Unless anyone's got something to raise, we'll get on with the line-up of animals booked in this morning.' He was looking at her as if he expected her to say something.

Just as well, because she and Finn did have an announcement to make. 'I have something to say.'

Finn leaned a little closer so his arm was against hers as he gave her a nod. They'd discussed this over breakfast that morning.

'Finn has moved back into my house. This time we're sharing the main bedroom.'

'Woohoo.'

'Awesome.'

'About time.' Peter grinned.

'That's great news, guys.'

Finn held up his hand. 'Wait, there's more.' His arm went round her waist, pulling her closer to his divine body. 'We're getting married in June and you're all invited.'

The congratulations coming from everyone filled the room with noise, and made Kate's heart swell with happiness. This was wonderful. These people had become such a part of her life and now they were sharing her and Finn's excitement. She held up her hand and called above the racket, 'But wait, there's still more to come.'

Slowly everyone quietened, watching her avidly. 'Come on, do tell.'

Kate glanced at Finn. The love in his eyes made her melt on the inside. 'Okay, here it is.

We are having a baby in late November. Watch this space. Oh, and this time you're not invited to the event.'

If Kate thought her news would be received quietly with a few lovely comments, she was wrong. The room exploded with laughter and she was being hauled to her feet for hugs from everyone. Finn was clapped on the back by the men and hugged by the women. She caught his eye and winked. Love you, she mouthed.

'Back at you,' he said.

Then Di held up her phone. 'Sorry, everyone, but we have an emergency. A cat versus puppy. Both need attention.'

Warmth spread throughout Kate. Nothing got in the way of helping sick or injured animals. This was her life and she had all she could possibly want. Her hand touched her abdomen, and she smiled. These days it was about the baby and nothing to do with the past. She and Finn had found their futures—together. She couldn't be happier if she tried.

* * * * *

*If you enjoyed this story,
check out these other great reads
from Sue MacKay*

Healing the Single Dad Surgeon
Paramedic's Fling to Forever
Marriage Reunion with the Island Doc
Resisting the Pregnant Pediatrician

All available now!